Praise for *Lucky T[icket]*

'Filled with distinctive characters and full of surprises,
these stories are enlightening and unforgettable.'
ALICE PUNG

'An exciting, profound and often funny dive into the
minor cataclysms of everyday life. Joey Bui is a marvel.'
BRAM PRESSER

'Joey Bui writes with a rare emotional acuity. Although her
characters inhabit very different lives, her stories are linked by a
searching quality, and by the assured clarity of her prose. *Lucky
Ticket* is meticulously observed and distinctly contemporary.'
JENNIFER DOWN

'After reading this devastatingly great collection—
imbued with equal parts pain and humour, suffering and the
sublime—I want to recommend it to not just my Vietnamese
or Asian-Australian friends, but anyone who reads.'
BENJAMIN LAW

'Joey Bui is a masterful storyteller. The stories in *Lucky Ticket*
are so diverse in setting and voice, it's hard to believe they were all
written by the same person. Each tale is delightfully rich with detail
and yet reverberates with a broader truth. When the book finished,
I was sad to leave its pages but heartened to know that such a
collection exists in the world. These unforgettable characters and
stories will keep me company for a gloriously long time.'
MELANIE CHENG

'A feast of stories—deliciously varied,
speaking true, speaking fierce, from every margin,
about what it means to be a part of life.'

TISHANI DOSHI
Author of *Small Days and Nights*

'Bui's sentences range over people and land battered
by war and movement. They tell you how and why people long
and love like wild things. They tell you hustlers bide their time,
dreamers too. Importantly, they tell you Bui's got game.'

DEEPAK UNNIKRISHNAN
Author of *Temporary People*, winner of the
Restless Books Prize for New Immigrant Writing

'The ways in which [the stories] delve into the indignity
of poverty call to mind Jenny Zhang, while the astute racial,
gender and class commentary would appeal to readers of
Julia Koh, Melanie Cheng and Rosanna Gonsalves.'

BOOKS+PUBLISHING

'Fanfare will herald this debut by a thrilling
new writer—and rightly so. These stories are finely
crafted, Bui's light touch revealing both confidence and
a keen sense for the right measure of mystery. Her characters
inhabit margins and she takes readers deep into lives that are
exquisitely unique, yet startlingly universal. Perhaps the most
exciting story here is that of Joey Bui's bright career ahead.
What a start! So now let there be fireworks, and let
her render them for us in her inimitable way.'

MIGUEL SYJUCO
Author of *Ilustrado*, winner of the Man Asian Literary Prize

LUCKY TICKET

Joey Bui is a Vietnamese-Australian writer. She graduated from New York University Abu Dhabi, where she completed her first collection of short stories, *Lucky Ticket*, based on interviews with Vietnamese refugees around the world. Joey has been published in journals and magazines in the US and Australia. She is currently studying at Harvard Law School.

LUCKY
382917

TICKET
382918

JOEY BUI
382919

TEXT PUBLISHING MELBOURNE AUSTRALIA

textpublishing.com.au

The Text Publishing Company
Swann House, 22 William Street, Melbourne Victoria 3000, Australia

First published in 2019 by The Text Publishing Company

Book design by Jessica Horrocks
Cover images by Michael Burrell/Alamy Stock Photo and iStock
Typeset by J&M Typesetting

Printed and bound in Australia by Griffin Press, part of the Ovato group, an accredited ISO/NZS 14001:2004 Environmental Management System printer

ISBN: 9781922268020 (paperback)
ISBN: 9781925774795 (ebook)

A catalogue record for this book is available from the National Library of Australia

For ông bà ngoại

Lucky Ticket

Fortunes rise and fall. One day you have a lucky ticket and get a dinner so good and you eat so much that you think you'll never need to eat again. You get busy making plans and then the hunger comes looking for you.

I'm just an old man selling lucky tickets, but my theory is that we all get our turn in the end. I've had my turn at fortune. It was some years ago, maybe 2002, because I remember that was when Sài Gòn was less red and bright with the fried chicken signs everywhere. Things were not as good, everything was dirty, dirtier than now. I didn't have this chair then, I was still walking around on my knuckles. See how they're so big and swollen? They never went back to normal.

That day in 2002 I walked over to Điện Phú Electronics, like I do every day. I try to do some business on the way. I passed the ladies selling *bánh cuốn* for breakfast, not very good ones, but I never said so, because sometimes one of them bought a ticket, with a little persuasion from me. That's a big part of my job, I smile and I laugh all day long. It makes people feel better, and they buy a ticket.

None of the ladies bought a ticket, but one gives me a *bánh cuốn* with the rice-paper skin broken. Like I said, not the best *bánh cuốn*, but how could I refuse? Because the skin was broken, the insides slipped out as I ate it. I wiped my chin and—*aiya!*—I flicked sauce onto somebody walking by. It was an Asian lady, but she had yellow hair. Bright yellow like the sun.

I didn't say anything because I was afraid of spitting more food onto her. She stared at me and I stared at her, still trying to chew up the *bánh cuốn*. She was strange-looking, her big oval eyes too far apart. A breeze came up and lifted all the yellow hair about her.

She leaned down, smelling like roses and lotions, and gave me a ticket, number 382918. 'Good luck,' she said.

You can't explain it any other way. I just knew it was my lucky ticket, number 382918. I put it my pocket.

I sold twenty tickets by the end of the afternoon. Thinking about this lucky ticket in my pocket, I couldn't keep it to myself anymore. I finished up early and walked down to find Hiếu, who was working in front of the blind school, to tell him the good news.

Hiếu is one of the smartest guys I've ever known. You know the Quốc Văn Giáo Khoa Thư lessons, the ones from school? He could recite them all, word for word. All the poems too, he knew them all. He could tell what any tree was before its fruit had grown. Hiếu had the problem a lot of smart guys have: no one liked him. He was also very fat, mostly in the face. His cheeks pushed up against his eyes and his neck bulged. Now that we were getting old, all the bulges drooped on him. And he was so black, like some of the French guys in the war.

Because of the way his cheeks were, Hiếu's speech was not good, so the poems always sounded weird coming out of him, with *b*s and *ph*s everywhere.

'*The beggar wanphs the sweeb gourd rice.*' That's what he sounded like.

'People care too much about what's on the outside, that's the problem with most people,' I'd tell Hiếu.

'We *are* the outside, Kiệt! We're always outside! So why don't they care about us!' he'd reply. I'm saying it without the accent so that you can understand. He was funny. I would be jealous if I wasn't his only friend in the world.

At night, we used to go and look at Notre Dame cathedral, Hiếu's favourite place in the city. That was before the police started banning beggars. We stood in the alleyway next to the Sài Gòn Post Office. Everything looked much brighter in the dark, the café lights and motorbike beams, the girls in lipstick. Hiếu would sing '*Chị Tôi*', 'My Sister'. His lisp wasn't so bad when he sang.

Many years have passed when I come back to my hometown
I see the leaves grown stale on the bridge
The shadow of my once beautiful sister
The shadow of a beauty never loved.

It was the saddest thing I'd ever known, listening to Hiếu sing '*Chị Tôi*'. It made me think that I'd do anything, anything, if only Hiếu could be in love. Nothing would be worth more to me than for him to be in love.

My theory is you can't feel very full without feeling sad, so it's necessary sometimes to scrape right down to the bottom. We went to Notre Dame so many times just to feel that sad.

I told him that I had a lucky ticket.

'Too good, too good!' Hiếu said. 'Will you finally get me a hooker?'

'I don't have the money yet.'

'What do you mean! What happened?'

'I just got the ticket, number 382918. I can't get the money until they announce the results on Thursday.'

'How much money do you have right now?'

I counted 30,000 đồng from that day, and 120,000 đồng I had saved up. It was just enough for the best seafood dinner you could imagine and a lot of beer. We went to a drinking stall on Thảo Điền. I gave the money to Hiếu so he could show it to the waitress. Because I don't have legs, I never get seated.

She picked up a stool for Hiếu and carried it to the back of the alleyway. We ordered plates and plates of snails, even the new fingernail snails that we hadn't seen before, grilled in garlic and soaked in scallion oil, and raw with lemon and pepper. But Hiếu ate and drank much more than me and then he threw it all up. I saw whole bits of snail meat as thick as my pinky. I wasn't happy about it, because I had paid a lot for this meal and Hieu hadn't even chewed it up properly. I can't stand it when I see or smell anyone else vomiting, so I vomited as well. It was very watery because of the beer, dotted with the green scallion, and all of it pooled under the table.

The manager came to kick us out, but Hiếu was too drunk to get up. He said something, but no one could tell what it was because of the grey snail-beer bubbles frothing at his mouth.

'Come on!' The manager pulled on the collar of Hiếu's shirt. But Hiếu was so heavy that he slipped and fell backwards. His head thudded on the pavement and the vomit spread a dark circle on his knee.

'Please,' I said, touching the manager's leg. 'My friend is sick.'

He turned to the waitress. 'Why are you serving these guys?'

'They had money.'

'We're just a couple of harmless old fools,' I said. 'Can I sell you a lucky ticket?'

'Look, how about this,' the manager said. 'I buy a couple of tickets from you, and you get out of here, okay? It's not good for my business. You understand.'

'Thank you, thank you. I'll sell you five lucky tickets, 4000 đồng. Bargain, last one free.'

The funny thing is, I gave him my lucky ticket, 382918, and I didn't know it until Hieu and I were sitting two streets away from the stall. I reached into my pocket for a feel, thinking that, despite the spoilt dinner, we still had the lucky ticket and the fortune coming. I rifled through the stack of tickets again, and felt hot spasms shooting up my throat. My tears leaked onto the wrong tickets.

'Hey, hey, captain, what's wrong?'

He called me captain because I always wore camouflage, and maybe because he was younger than me. But it was camouflage from the Cambodian war, not the Vietnam war, and I was only a foot soldier.

'I gave him my lucky ticket, 382918,' I sobbed.

'No, no, no, no, no!' he wailed.

Hiếu took the stack of tickets, soggy with tears, and spread them out on the pavement in a grid pattern. I watched him examine the number on each one. As he bent over the tickets, his huge belly hung down like a bag. He looked like a very clever and famous gambler laying out his cards. I think I recognised him from a past life. He must be paying now for great greed in his past.

'You're right,' he said finally. 'There is no 382918.'

'What do we do?' I slumped down and the tin garage door of the clock shop behind me rattled.

Hiếu rolled over onto his bottom and pushed himself up with determination.

'I'm going to get it back,' he said.

He was no longer drunk. He still had that look on his face, the ticket-counting look. He reached down and shook me by the shoulders. 'They have stolen too much from you. I have to get it back!' he said, and his grip tightened so much that it hurt.

He was fearsome for a moment before he lumbered away, back down the road, to pay the debt he owed from his past.

I stayed in front of the clock shop, waiting for him to come back. I waited all night. In the morning, a lot of the tickets Hiếu had laid out in a grid pattern had dried and blown away. The rest were stuck to the pavement. The clock shop manager came at 6am and made me mop the front of his shop. I mopped and left the tickets in a dumpster before I left. I never saw Hiếu again, not in front of the blind school or anywhere.

But my theory is that nothing disappears forever. Nothing really goes away. You'll see when I tell you what happened next.

I went back to my corner in front of Điện Phú and I stayed patient. On the good days I made 40,000 đồng and I ate well. Other days I got a packet of gum and I sat chewing and massaging my leg stumps, just thinking about how hungry I was, so hungry that I forgot to do anything else. Other days I can't remember what I did. One day I met Lượng, who offered me a job.

Lượng had to clean the toilets at the petrol station on Nguyễn Thơ, where he also pumps. He came to my spot in front of Điện Phú Electronics in a sort of panic, although I soon found out that he always spoke like that, like a cockroach in the corner with a shoe coming for him.

'I can't bend my neck, see, it's a condition I've always had. I can't look down,' he said. It was true, he couldn't look at me when he spoke. Even though he squatted down to talk to me, he couldn't bend his neck to look up either.

It made him look crazy. I'm not saying this because I mind appearances—you know I don't mind what people look like. But it was a shame for him because he was a young man—I think he was about twenty-eight when I met him—and needed to be looking for a wife. He also smelled like petrol all the time.

'So when I reach down to clean the toilets, I can't look at where I'm reaching and I keep getting shit all up and down my arms. I was thinking you could do it better, because, you know.'

He glanced at my stumps.

'To be honest,' he continued, 'I feel sorry for vets like you, you really got screwed over, okay? I want to look out for you because you lost out so much, and I see the VC guys in their nice three, four-storey houses. I'm not saying anything about politics, that's not what I mean, but everybody sees it.'

He winced.

'Look, where do you sleep?'

So that I could clean the toilets every day, Lượng offered me some space in the house where he stayed in the Trung Bình projects.

All of a sudden my life changed without me even trying. It was a kind of good fortune. On the first night, I drew the curtain shut and everything was dark and hushed. There was something about being kept inside like that, pretending there was a great space between my body and the world outside. It felt precious. I will never be able to repay Lượng for a thing like that.

In the morning, he drove me on his motorbike to the petrol station, talking the whole way.

'I know how I look, I know I look dark and skinny, but I'm actually very clever. I watch things, you see. The way people deal with each other, for example. If you praise a person a little bit, act like their friend, they're gonna have a hard time saying no to you. You have to do a bit of acting.'

The work was not bad. I am not squeamish about the things young men are squeamish about. Lượng was right, cleaning the latrines was easier for me because of my stumps. But I had to walk on my knuckles and so the shit got all over my hands and arms. But I didn't mind. People are washable, I always say.

Most nights after work I waited at the petrol station and Lượng came along later, smelling of beer and grumpy about something.

'I'm a very hard worker,' he said on the ride back to Trung Bình. 'I am always working, even when you think I'm not. I'm working people. When I'm drinking with someone, I'm meeting a possible business partner, see? But success doesn't come right away. You have to work and work. Please people, please them. When I become rich, every one of my relatives will be shocked by the great gifts I have for them.'

He was really a boring guy. But in my time with Lượng, I ate every day. Sometimes I shopped while I waited for him in the evenings. I bought blankets from the ladies selling on the corner of Nguyễn Thơ and, one time, I bought a little toy dog with a battery inside. He could bark if I turned on a switch underneath him, but I never did because it would have been too noisy in the house.

In the summer, Lượng met a girl, Phụng, who also lived in the Trung Bình projects. I remember it was summer because, all night long, Phụng hissed through the curtains about how hot it was.

'Fuck my mother, I can't stand this heat. Get up, get up, get your body away from me. I can't stand your fucking disgusting skin touching me and your pores full of pus leaking all over my skin.'

During sex was the only time Phụng didn't talk, only grunted. Afterwards, she would exhale with disgust and talk about how repulsive the sex was. Some nights it was a softer pleading.

'Please, please, stay away from me. Please. I feel sick.'

I listened to her as I drifted in and out of sleep. Sometimes she sobbed between hisses. The curtains were thin and I felt as if her voice was all around me.

Later in the summer, she started to include me in her ramblings, speaking about me from the other side of the curtains. 'I bet he's diseased. Have you seen his hair? Don't you see the disease caked on his skin? Have you seen the way he stares at me? He's mad, I promise you he's mad. He's going to kill us in the middle of the night, you have no idea.'

My skin crawled every night she was there; I imagined bugs crawling out of her, the tiny yellow kind, the ones you sometimes see flitting through the air and you're not sure if they're dust or not.

From her voice, I guessed Phụng must have been about

sixteen. I never saw her. She always came late at night when the curtains were already drawn. Sometimes I watched the girls walk around the projects and tried to guess which one was Phụng, but every girl seemed as sour-looking as the next, and I began imagining different faces for each night of hissing.

I did a lot of thinking around that time, because I wasn't able to sleep. I felt afraid everywhere I went, and I didn't exactly know why. I was afraid of making a noise, of moving, of disturbing someone.

One night I was riding on the back of Lượng's motorbike as he crossed the city for a meth order. I saw the lights of Notre Dame between buildings and my vision swam with the glare of the dazzling shopfronts and the bright blue-and-white electronics stores. The soft chatter of the city folk sounded almost like another language.

I began to sing.

Many years have passed since we last saw him, the bridge has finished building
My sister waits until her eyes glaze over cold
New fruits grow on the bridge and fall down one by one
My sister is still not loved.

I had never liked my singing voice, but that night I was moved by the sound of it.

'Stop singing or I'll throw you off the bike,' Lượng said.

I remembered the old sadness, the scrape-to-the-bottom sadness that Hieu and I used to go out to Notre Dame for. I felt a sort of flowing feeling in my chest, like my heart would flood, and I was struck by the idea that it was love's kind of sadness, that this day was the best I had lived in a long time.

When I sang the next line, the inside of my mouth pooled with spit.

My sister is still not loved.

'What the fuck? Are you crying?' Lượng jerked his shoulder irritably.

I was startled. I gulped. My hands slipped off the metal bars and I sailed out onto my back. My neck arched and I saw a swirl of coloured clothes and frightened faces just as my head hit the pavement. Then pain clouded my vision and filled my head with sharp green and red lights. I couldn't move.

Here is what I remember: a gentle, pale yellow colour everywhere, something soft on my face, like freshly crushed mung beans. It was surrounding me, and yet it didn't feel strange. I was serene.

I couldn't see through the mung beans, but heard voices close to my face, as though there were lips about to brush my cheeks.

'Who is it?'

The voice was clear and deep. I imagined the face of an old king. When he paused, there was a marvellous silence. I miss that silence most of all. It was how I knew I was in the heavens, where the dirty chatter of humans had finished.

'I think we have made a mistake,' said the king.

There was a series of knocks.

'What do you want to do?' said a second voice.

'Has he found fortune?' the king asked.

'Not in this life. We can move him on.'

The king hummed deep in his throat, the way wise men do when they're thinking. After a long time, he spoke. 'Has she come yet? She has to find him.'

More knocking sounds.

'Let him go back,' the king said.

The yellow mung beans blanketed my eyes. I felt so relaxed and knew I was going to sleep.

When I came to, I was at the top of a building, in a hammock that was tied to the bars of a balcony. Down the corridor, there were bodies lying on stretchers, silent and bruised. It was a hospital. I had never been in a hospital before.

Thick gauze was wrapped around my head, which hurt at the back, so I rolled onto my side. I reached down. My stumps were also bandaged. I massaged them as I looked at the people around me. Next to me, a man was hanging his clothes out to dry. I felt great optimism in my heart and wanted to connect with him.

'Hello, young man!' I said.

He turned around. He wore glasses and his glossy black hair flopped down the right side of his face. 'Greetings, uncle.' He smiled.

'You look well,' I said.

'You sure as hell don't.' He chuckled, then immediately looked very tired. He turned back to his wet clothes.

'Then I'm in the right place, aren't I? What are you doing here?'

'Waiting for the long road to death.' He turned to face me. 'Would you believe it, I've been sleeping in this hospital two nights already, just waiting to pay my wife's hospital bill.'

I thought of the hospital bill. It was Lượng's revenge, I knew, taking me to the hospital and leaving me there, unable to pay.

'Two days? Why so long?'

His forehead pinched with concern. It made him look like a handsome, wise man. A young man's face with the seriousness of age. He looked how I imagined the young Vietnamese musicians, like Trần Tiến, looked when they lived alone in Russia.

'Paperwork takes so long in this place,' he said. He pointed. 'You see the people lying in the corridor? Some have been sleeping here over a week to pay hospital bills for their family.'

I looked left and right, and the differences between patients and their caretakers became clearer. Caretakers were fully clothed, and clutched plastic bags as they slept or stared out into the courtyard.

'They come from Bến Tre, from Tây Ninh, faraway villages, these poor peasants with no other choice. The temple monks serve food outside the hospital, but only four days a week. The other three they have to beg for it in the hospital.'

I thought for a moment. 'Why don't you just pay when your turn comes?'

'Would we sleep here if we knew when our turn was coming? We have to be ready at any time or else they fuck up the treatment. They bruise your wife's arm when they inject her, they miss a day's medication, they let an infection fester a little longer. They charge an extra bribe fee, you know, so it can't go into any books or anything. You get the idea.'

'What's wrong with your wife?' I asked.

'Machine ate up her hand. She worked in a cardboard factory.'

'Ate up?'

'Oh yeah, her skin ripped right off the bone. It's foul, but don't say anything to her. She hates it when I tell people, but how could they not notice anyway when she's got no hand?'

I laughed, a slow, dry wheeze at first, and then great roars that surprised me. It had been a while since I'd used my voice properly.

He smiled again. 'You should have seen her when she first got here. Fucking disgusting.' His voice rose in excitement. 'They cut a slit in her stomach and she had to sit with her hand in there—inside her stomach!—so that the flesh could grow around the bone. Keep it fresh, you know, until they could sew on some skin from her backside.'

I laughed until my head felt light.

'So how about you?' he said. He glanced at my stumps.

'I fell off a bike.'

'Onto a meat cleaver?'

'No, no. This is old, from the war.' I touched my right stump.

'Cộng Hòa?'

'Yeah.'

He nodded. He started eyeing his pile of wet clothes again, but I wanted to keep talking.

'Fucking Chinese, huh?' I said.

He swung some pant legs—white with purple dots, surely a woman's pants—over the balcony bars next to me. 'What?'

'The Chinese bombs, right? You don't know?' I chuckled, trying to match his tone. I grabbed onto my left stump with both hands. 'This is the handiwork of the Chinese, this is. They think hard about what they want their bombs to do. They don't want to kill you, see. Because who are you? No one. They got their own billion people they kill all the time. They're better than that.'

I had him.

'The Chinese bombs don't explode *up*, they explode low so that they take your legs. Only your legs! One hundred Vietnamese soldiers run through a field and *umph, umph, umph, umph!*'

I smacked one fist into the other palm for each bomb.

'Two hundred legs fly off! You are ruined, you cannot fight them anymore, but you still have to keep living. You become a burden to Vietnam, one more cripple to look after. You see? You get it?'

An old nurse came down the hallway. She was large, sweaty, and encased in a tight faded-pink uniform. 'What's all the noise?' she said.

'I'm talking to the old vet here,' my companion replied.

'Don't you have something better to do?' she snapped.

'I've been waiting two days to pay for my wife's surgery, ma'am, and the doctors won't give her a check-up until I do,' he said.

16

'You make any more trouble and I won't give her any anaesthesia.'

She turned around to face me. 'You're a vet?' she asked. She eyed my stumps. 'Who authorised you to be here?'

'I just woke up,' I muttered.

She reached up and tugged at my head gauze. 'Do you have any idea how expensive this is? How are you going to afford it? Fuck my mother, looking at you makes my eyes sore,' she said, and continued down the corridor.

As she walked away, my friend chuckled. 'But the Vietnamese don't take care of their cripples anyway, that's their trick. Well, not the soldiers on our side anyway,' he said.

I felt a rush of warmth at the words 'our side'.

'You'd think there would be good people here,' he said.

'Everybody's just looking to eat,' I said.

'You better be gone before she comes back.'

'What? I can't leave,' I said.

'It's easy. They don't even know who to stop. Just leave,' he said.

'I can't, I can't,' I said, starting to feel anxious.

'You will be in debt to the hospital for the rest of your life. Sorry to be honest, uncle, but I don't think you can pay for it, can you? It's okay. Leaving is the only thing you can do,' he said.

Even though I was terrified, I wanted to listen to him. He had the kind and dishevelled air of a scholar. A lot like you.

'I have to go too, so I don't see you run away,' he said. He offered me his hand. 'I'm Cường. Good luck, old man.'

'Kiệt,' I said. Then I thought about saying 'wait' but no sound left my mouth.

He started to walk away and I panicked. I had to move. It took me a long time to reach the stairs, but no one stopped me. I turned around.

'Go, go!' Cường shouted.

I lurched as fast as I could on my hands, afraid of every person watching. Once I got through the dark corridors of concrete, past the tired relatives in plastic chairs, clutching bags, and the booths of unhappy secretaries filling out endless forms—once I got through it all and reached the street, I realised that I hadn't been free at all before, and that now I was. I laughed and laughed and laughed so I would remember it well.

The truth is, I'm a fearful old man. What good fortune it was that I met Cường. I'm not foolish enough to believe that was an accident. I'm a fearful old man with a touch of good fortune.

We are the outside, I heard Hiếu saying in my head. What a change I felt in myself then. I believe that it is too easy to forget to live while you are doing other things. You chase morsels of food, one after the other, and then one day you realise that you have lost your way. I had gone too far from my path of fortune. Hiếu had come back to tell me so. Do you understand? Do you see? He was not gone forever.

I walked all the way down to Bến Thành market to find Nam, the seafood supplier who used to sell me tickets. The market rumbled with voices, snapping and whining theatrically as the good people bargained. That is what the Vietnamese do best.

Nam was perched on his stall, squatting over a little wooden bench, scraping squid clean with a metal blade.

'Look who it is!' he burst out. Because of my good mood, everything about him and the market seemed heavenly. The gleaming white squid rested smoothly in his fat palm. The water in which he dipped the squid was clear—Nam prided himself on the cleanliness of his produce. Buckets in front of him were filled to spilling, one with rounds of blushing pink basa amongst ice shards, others with mottled eel and shrimp and sucker barb. In a deeper tub, live crabs were scratching their pincers, fidgeting over one another and splashing in the water.

Nam dropped his blade and flapped his hands to dry them. 'Where have you been, captain?' he asked. 'I was hoping hard as hell. I said to myself, I hope the old man didn't die. I must love you a little bit, don't you think!'

'I don't know where I've been, Nam,' I said. 'I think I was foolish, chasing the wrong fortune.'

'I know how it is, exactly how it is.' He sighed, tipping his head down to rest on his double chin. 'Are you well? What's that on your head?'

'A bad accident.'

At the same moment, he clapped his large palms together. I couldn't tell if he had heard me.

'Look, I want to help you, captain,' he said, suddenly grave. He leaned over to rest his forearms on his knees. 'But you never paid me back for the tickets from last time.'

I glanced down at the buckets, afraid he would fall into them. 'I lost them.'

'What do you mean, lost?'

'Gone, just gone.'

'This is bad, uncle.' He sighed again. 'I can't waste tickets just because you decide to run off after a fortune. You know I'm a good man. I'm an honest businessman.'

'You won't waste any more tickets. I'm not going to leave. I'm going to keep selling tickets for good,' I said.

'Maybe we'll just start with fifty. That okay? Do you have any money on you now?'

'No.' Everything was back at the Trung Bình projects. The blanket, the soaps, the toy dog, a change of camouflage, and about 200,000 đồng.

Nam sighed again. He rummaged in some pouches by his feet and I glimpsed wads of blue 20,000-đồng notes packed inside, thick and clean. He pulled out a bunch of tickets bound by a rubber band.

'You'll be back?' he asked, as he handed over the bunch.

'I swear.'

'You know I'm a good man,' he said again.

'I do.'

'All right. All right, captain.' He patted my hand. 'Take care of your health.'

We settled back into our rhythm. I sold tickets on the corner of Điện Phú Electronics and at the end of the week I went to the fish market to pay my debt to Nam. I didn't see Lượng again. The *bánh cuốn* ladies told me there were two rumours, one that I had died and the other that I had gone to my ancestral home in Bến Tre to die. Little did they know that I had already died. I made sure to ask the *bánh cuốn* ladies if they remembered the lady with yellow hair.

'Don't be difficult, captain, there are so many women with yellow hair. It's a bleach dye, very easy,' Sister Minh scolded.

I couldn't explain what was unique about the lady I had seen. I didn't have the words. How could I return to my path to good fortune? After the dream, I knew that the lady had come to give me my fortune. I remember as clear as day the light about her and the way I knew instantly that she was giving me a lucky ticket. But how could I find her?

One morning, I was in front of Điện Phú Electronics as usual. Two men were standing outside the store, one of them smoking. They were well dressed and had come with their wives, who were inside the store. Việt Kiều, the Vietnamese boat people who now lived abroad. I don't know why I didn't offer them some tickets; I usually approach anybody passing by.

After a while, the smoker came over to me.

'You don't happen to be a Cộng Hòa veteran?' He was very polite.

I touched my camouflage, smiling.

He had a cheerful face, dark-skinned although he was a Việt Kiều, who are usually pale. The Việt Kiều also have a certain posture that sets them apart. Their spine is straight, their shoulders back.

'Yes, yes, I am, sir. Are you visiting, sir?' I said.

'I'm visiting family.' He gestured to the other man, who looked around with polite interest. 'I said to my friend that you must be a Cộng Hòa veteran. The VC wouldn't leave behind one of their own like this.'

'Cộng Hòa, platoon Seven A,' I said.

'Seven A? I think—' He paused and appealed to his friend again, who had turned away to smoke. 'I think that's my father's platoon! Well, I think it might be.'

'Are you sure, man?' his friend said.

Then I looked hard at the Việt Kiều's face, and suddenly remembered the same hollow cheeks on a face so thin that the skin sagged.

'Lộc!' I exclaimed.

He saw my recognition, and it was as if the ghost of my old friend was staring out of the eyes of this very thin, younger man.

'Yes, yes! Lộc, yes!' he said.

'Văn Minh Lộc,' I said. Sudden joy leaped into my soul and I knew that I had been right all along about the feeling of the cycle, of everything living on and moving around, and it was so sweet to feel the truth of the world that day.

I took the man's hands so that he would come closer to me. 'My friend Lộc,' I said, crying. 'Oh, where is he?'

The man looked at me so seriously that I think he may also have recognised the sweetness of immortality.

'I am Phước, his son,' he said. 'My father died about ten years ago.'

Of course I knew that Lộc had already died, otherwise I

would not have seen his eyes through this man right then. Now, years later, I wonder how it was that a well-fed Việt Kiều was still as skinny and starved as Lộc and I were in the war…

'What do you remember about my father?'

'I remember everything,' I said.

Now both of the Việt Kiều men were listening to me intently.

I told them about the first time I thought Lộc and I were going to die. Our squad of ten was sent to the outskirts of the city Long Khánh. It was a strange mission because no one knew who would meet us there and our captain got angry when we asked him for details. I had the feeling all along that there would be no end of the road, no Point B. I was very good with these things; back then I knew many things without having to think about them, only by witnessing them several times already.

'Long Khánh wasn't far,' I told Phước now. 'We were dropped off at Giang Điền and we walked the rest of the way, to a deserted stone house in Long Khánh. The grass around the house was unkempt and wet; there was no farmland in sight. It felt like the wrong place, and I sensed that we had come exactly where the enemy had planned for us to come.

'"The map is wrong," I said to the other men. "We were given the wrong map."

'They began to disagree, but there was no point. We decided that it was easier to start walking back in the morning.

'We sat in the house with the doors open and took off our shoes, which were always damp because of the wetlands.

'"Do you smell the lake?" said Xuân, a particularly dreamy man, the youngest among us.

'"What lake?"

'"We are close to Hồ Trị An, an enormous lake in the middle of the country, between the sea and the mountain. My cousins live nearby and when we visited them for Tết, we went fishing and swimming in the lake. You can look down the length of it and the width and you can't see where it ends. It's a real country picture, like in thread paintings."

'At one point during the night, we heard scuffling. We went outside to investigate, staring into the distance at the grass and the road. In the space between wondering and knowing that there were foot soldiers bearing down on us, the dread settled into my stomach. When I looked at the others, I saw the fear in Xuân's face. He lifted his rifle before any of us could think to say anything.

'*BAM!* He shot, and immediately, *immediately,* the fire was returned.

'I slapped the unused newspaper box next to me and the metal rattled.

'They were waiting, they were ready! You have to admit, wow, they were ready for us.

'We ran. No one, not even the corporal, took charge, no orders. They were using B40s, B41s, the rifles with bullets this big, and long like this, that could blow up a whole Jeep in one go. They probably thought there were more of us. And they started moving up, see, I might have been some five, six metres away from them. Two of our soldiers were shot dead. Right there.

'I crawled over to the bank and rolled down into a rice paddy. I started crawling through the water, then lay down still. When they came in, they ran along the path right past me. I could have waved an arm and touched a VC! It is enough to make you piss your pants. Lộc had come out with me and he was lying on the other side of this branch of the ô rô tree, you know the kind that only grows in water?

'I looked at Lộc. We had dead calm faces, because we knew if we got worked up they would kill us on the spot. We lay there in the water, not moving, for a long time, after the last VC had gone. I lay there until my stomach felt all right again. We needed time to get from fear to love for our lives and our good fortune. I've always been lucky like that. I always come out with my life.

'When I looked at Lộc's face again, it was his love for life that I saw. And I felt it too, all over my skin. It tingled, you see. Being alive is so sweet, but I don't always remember it like that. You keep forgetting things like that when you are as old as I am. Not the details—I remember all the details. But the truth, oh, it slips and slips and slips all the time. I get so distracted.'

I'm telling you almost exactly as I told them.

I remembered all of this so well because I had suddenly seen Lộc's face again in his son's and, now that I come to think of it, Lộc's face was so important to me in the war. It was the face I saw at all the important moments.

The Việt Kiềus were moved by my story. Lộc's son Phước

beamed the whole way through, even during the bad moments, when the two kids in our squad died.

'Why are you still here, uncle? Why didn't you take the H1 visa with all the other Cộng Hòa soldiers and go to America?' he asked.

'Oh, I couldn't. I could never have done that.'

'Why? Your life must be so hard here,' he said with emotion.

'I couldn't leave, no. I'm not the kind of person to do that.'

He looked affronted. 'What kind of…What do you mean?' A flash of impatience crossed his face.

'That's not what I mean, son.' He had already called me uncle, which I accepted. 'I have nothing against the Việt Kiều. Please believe me. What I mean is…'

Phước looked like he really needed to know, so I thought long and hard.

'The truth is that I'm a fearful old man. I had already lost my legs when the war ended and I was so, so tired all the time. It was so hard for me to move anywhere, and the strain of having to ask people to help me get places… And it was not a good time for anyone to help anyone else. The Americans had just left; all the people in the South had to decide how to take care of their families, especially with all the Cộng Hòa soldiers leaving as well. We didn't know what the VC would do to us.

'Asking for somebody's help…When I feel something, I feel it with my whole body. I can feel a question with my whole body, and I could not, could not ask for help anymore. Everyone was too worried about other things. Everyone was leaving. There was an offer of H1 paperwork at some

26

point, but I couldn't do it. And they didn't want me for the re-education camps; they didn't bother taking the cripples. Everything just moved on.'

Then I didn't really want to talk to them anymore—it was getting too hard, and Phước was upset.

'But, uncle, would it have been different if my father had seen you like this? Have other soldiers come to Vietnam and seen you?' asked Phước.

'I was recognised once, but it is so long ago now.'

'It could be so different for you.'

The women had finished their shopping and come outside. Phước introduced them to me.

'This is Uncle Kiệt. He was a friend of my father's in the war.' The muscles in Phước's face seemed to contract all of a sudden. Those hollow cheeks now made him look as though he was about to yell.

The women fussed a little and asked some questions. Then they all bought a lot of tickets from me and left.

So many people pass me on the street. How can I explain myself to each one? I have been alive so long like this, it isn't good for me to ask myself, 'What if things were different?'

Two days later, as I sat on my corner, Phước came to see me again. At first I felt annoyed because the last time had left a stale taste in my mouth.

He walked around me frantically, as though deciding where he should stand. Then he knelt down.

'Uncle Kiệt,' he said.

'Phước, have you come here just to see me?'

'I thought about you, uncle, and I wanted to give you this.' He took a white envelope out of his pocket and handed it to me.

It would have been rude for me to look inside.

'It's a...it's something to help you a little,' he said. 'You could get a chair.'

He looked so uncomfortable, I wasn't sure if he had given me too much or too little. Việt Kiều are usually such big spenders. Some have paid 50,000 đồng for a ticket. I never pester anyone. I always ask once, and I stop working when I have enough for the day. I am never greedy.

He stared at me, as if wanting something from me, but I did not know what it was. Eventually he stood up.

'Take care, uncle. Perhaps I will come by and see you another time.'

Would you believe it? There was ten million đồng in that envelope. I had never held 500,000-đồng notes in my life. When he left and I finally opened the envelope, in front of Điện Phú Electronics, I immediately felt in danger. But, of course, I also felt joy! There would be good meals and things to buy and keep. But it was dangerous to walk around with ten million in your hands. I tensed up in fear, because it was a new experience to have something that other people wanted.

I decided to keep it in my pocket. If my body wasn't safe, there would be little use for the money anyway.

Nothing happened for a while, all the activity on my street seemed the same and I felt all right. I had time to think about what a large amount of money it was. And I had to think about how it was that good fortune was coming to me.

Do you remember all the good things in your life? Did they not come suddenly from nowhere, so that it frightened you and it hardly seemed like fortune then because it was yours? I'm trying to make you understand, because you are young and it is easy to miss many things when you are young. The money came suddenly into my life, so suddenly that it did not belong to me. Money does not belong to anyone. It is for passing on.

Only a day after I had this money—one day!—somebody came chasing after it. I was sitting on my corner, thinking about how to use it to change my life, when a large woman approached me, closer and closer, until she had her large, ruddy face right down in front of mine. I was shocked, especially by the way her eyes strained, as if trying to leave their sockets.

She was middle-aged and wore a bright-blue floral blouse that puffed out at her waist. Her hair was pulled tight and bunched at the back like the market women's hair.

'*Aaah*,' she moaned, her head shaking. '*Aaah*.'

It was as if we had been in a long conversation, at the end of which something puzzling had been made clear to her. She shook her head violently.

'*Aaah*, do you know who I am? *Do you know who I am?*' she cried. She stomped her right foot, and I looked down at the cartoon cat on her red rubber slipper. '*Do you know who I am?*'

I looked back up at her face and was struck by fear. I had never seen her before. Why was she putting on such a show?

29

'*Lâm Hùng Kiệt*,' she said. '*Lâm Hùng Kiệt*, I am your daughter.' She stared at me wildly.

'No, I don't know you.'

'It's true! Yes, yes.' She smiled broadly, her one-lidded eyes puffy. 'My name is Vy. Lâm Nhật Vy. Yes, yes, Nhật. I am Nhật's daughter,' she said. Now she was sobbing furiously. 'Thank the heavens I have found you at last. I am sorry it took so long. But oh, has it been hard for you? You look like you have suffered. But I am so happy to find you.'

She stared at me through her tears.

'Why don't you say something?' she cried out indignantly.

'I don't know you!'

'You don't know me yet. You were already in the army when I was born. But I *am* your daughter!'

She hiccupped violently and her enormous body shook. Bent over, her right knee on the ground, she lost her balance and slumped sideways.

'Father—'

'No! I don't know you.'

She lunged at me, and I fell back in terror.

'Please! Please, I don't know you.'

'*What*? What did you say? I'm Nhật's daughter. Nhật, your wife!' Her crying intensified. 'How could you not? I'm your daughter!'

'I don't know you.'

Her theatrics were so overwhelming that it took me until that moment to realise that the stranger was after my money.

'How has it come to this!' she cried out. To my surprise,

she struck her own face with the flat of her hand. She wailed and struck her face again and again. Then she stopped to stare at me. 'What suffering, I can't bear it! It breaks my heart to see you like this.'

She sounded possessed, clutching her chest as she shrieked, her purple-painted nails garish against her pale skin.

'What we have lost. What has been spoiled. Oh, oh, oh! How I have failed you. I will be punished for letting you live like this, my father, oh, my father. We have all been punished.'

'Enough!' I shouted. 'Don't you know that you cannot go on any longer? Enough!'

She clutched at my shirt. 'Will you not believe me? Will you come with me even if you do not believe me?' she said, subdued now. She sniffed loudly and wiped her face. 'I can take care of you. Let me take care of you. You can rest.'

'No, no, enough.' I backed away, so her hands could no longer reach me.

She was lying on the pavement, sobbing quietly. There was nothing to be done. I headed off.

I admit it took me a long time to be rid of the shock and discomfort of the encounter. I kept walking and walking, my knuckles aching, afraid she might follow me. I walked until I felt all right again. I walked until I realised that if I forgot the whole incident, it could not touch me anymore. I walked until the fear was gone.

The wealthiest beggars in Vietnam put on the best theatrics. It is very common. Babies are rented out to ambitious beggars. A whole troupe is very compelling—mother, baby, and young children. Especially a little girl, if she has a pretty face. And if she has wild stories to tell, and is good at crying and wailing.

I have never meddled in that business. No, I am content selling tickets because it is not dishonest. It is an exchange. Any man or woman who buys a lucky ticket for 7000 đồng from me may win the fifteen billion prize. Perhaps the woman was sent to me, right after Phước gave me the envelope, to remind me of my place and keep me humble. Money does not belong to anyone.

It was as though I had to be taught the lesson over and over again. Nothing sinks in. Wasn't that what I was telling you? The truths are so hard to remember. They slip all the time. There is nothing to be figured out, no mystery to fathom. The truth is all the time trying to explain itself to us, and we insist on forgetting. In school, we are made to remember and recite the lessons, but that is because it is so hard for us to hold onto them. How many times have I gone astray and been put back on my path?

I became angry at myself. I'm an old man, but I have made the same mistake, chasing after dumb fortunes, over and over, like a child.

I'm telling you because people don't listen to me, but they might listen to you. Can you tell everyone, the Việt Kiều where you live, not to forget people like me? Don't forget what we did and how we stayed behind.

My theory is that we all get our turn in the end. Look at how young you are, and the way you got to grow up. Look how pretty you are. I wonder how much you will pay for that. Or how much you have already paid for it. Me, I have nothing to be afraid of. *Hahaha!* Nothing at all. Right here I'm safe.

Did you get everything you need? Shall we stop here? You can always find me here if you need me. If I'm alive, I'm here, every day. If I'm not here, you'll know that I'm dead. *Ha!*

Hey, Brother

It's so hot—could you please reduce the heat from the fire a little? I would do it myself, but I see you are good with the logs and the twigs.

I believe that a person's soul is revealed in their hands. Do you agree? I think so when I see your hands touching the bark, rolling it so that the logs collapse just right, as though you know the grooves of each piece and how they should fit together. Look at your hands, pulling out that log now as it spits glowing coals, flipping it onto the sand. What a lovely way to spend a night in the Vietnamese countryside.

One day you might see the soul emerge when I play a

piano. You have never seen a piano, but they have them in the cafés of Sài Gòn. Grand cafés with live music at night and always a woman singer, with long hair, singing slow songs. Last week I was in such a café, down a side street not far from Dinh Độc Lập, the Independence Palace. The street was full of alleyways, bars with loud music, and street food.

Listen to me rattling on. Why don't you recline in this hammock opposite mine, and I shall call my old aunt to bring us some wine and squid to roast over the fire? Her husband, your boss, was sitting with me, but he is an inexperienced drinker and went to bed after two cups of wine. But you look like a sturdier man, with an excellent round stomach. Stay put and I will be right back with our food and drink.

Let us toast—what shall we toast to? Let us toast to this beautiful country! You must drink it all in one go. Look, it is not so hard. This is top-quality squid from Đà Nẵng. Shall we stick it onto some skewers? I suppose we can just leave them to cook on this log jutting out here. Or will they get covered in ash? Never mind, I will eat anything, I have a strong stomach. I have no qualms about eating the street food here. Many of my *ngoại quốc*, 'overseas Vietnamese', friends would feel queasy at the thought of those street dishes. I would happily eat the plates of fried flour cakes with the minced pork, squid sauce, carrots, and fried onion on top. I have an old female friend from high school, who wakes up early to cook the breakfast and lunch fare for commuters. She sells from six to nine in the morning, on the side of the street just before the turn-off to the highway. Little bags of rice and braised vegetables. Very convenient.

Now that we are comfortable and the squid is smoking nicely, what questions do you have for me? I know you must have questions, because it is not often that you meet a man like me in a small village like this. Are there any *ngoại quốc* in your family? I thought not. I am only here for a few days to pay my respects to my old aunt and uncle, which I am happy to do, of course. I have a very high regard for family. And I enjoy helping however I can. For example, yesterday I bought thirty sacks of rice to give to families in the village neighbourhood. What I mean to say is—let me pour some more wine for you—this little fishing town is not a common spot for visitors and I can open up the world for people like you.

Can you please reduce the heat of the fire a little more? Thank you. Let me tell you about my home in Paris, in the 13th arrondissement. I can show you where it is on my phone. If I my pinch my fingers like so, we can see deep into Paris, to the very streets and small parks. This is my apartment, on Rue Damesme, right there. There are five apartments to a floor here. It is not very big, but that does not make it less valuable. Property in Paris is more about location than space and we are in a very good location. We are right by the hospital and the Parc de Choisy. There is even a *phở* restaurant nearby, called Ba Miền. The French enjoy *phở* very much. In fact Ba Miền is often full of white people! It shows that my Paris is a very generous society and, like I told you, my French friends think that I may as well be one of them.

I also own a property in the suburbs in Vitry-sur-Seine. It is a real house, free-standing, and I rent it out because that's a very smart way to make money. You have to be smart like this. The immigrant must not be lazy, as I sometimes see the local youths are here, loitering and begging on the streets. It is a symbol of the decline of our country. I've seen it coming a long time. It is insulting to see my people living idle lives, lying around in hammocks, expecting somebody else to feed them. And the rich youths too, who will never do anything of value because of their corrupt fathers and grandfathers, who work for the government. I spit on the Communist dogs. What? Do you think the Việt Cộng are hiding behind the banks of that irrigation stream, which is dry and full of dead fish? You should be so lucky.

Nobody works anymore. Only the Americans. They build those KFCs, with their fried chicken and white tiles, in our country, and the rich kids are there on the second floor, eating American chicken as though their mothers never had chicken at home. I want to know what they put in the American chickens that are turning everybody fat and lazy. But what choice do we have? The Chinese chickens are even worse. They are stuffed with bits of plastic. I read it in a newspaper once. What about the Vietnamese chickens, I ask you? Where are they? I suppose there are a million Vietnamese chickens running all over the country and nobody wants to eat them.

Are you sure you don't want more wine? I see you are not used to the taste. Wine is something you have to learn, like numbers, like words. It has to be understood. But it isn't the wine. I can see in your eyes what is the matter. You think I do not know, but I know. I am just like you, my brother. We are bitter. Not long ago, I was living in a small, dirty village like this one.

Although my family, as you know, is better than yours. So I made myself study and I was accepted into a sports-coaching course at the university in Sài Gòn. There I was, studying with other young people. But the war ended, the Communists won, and I had to leave my country, my family and friends, my home and my life—everything—and escape by sea. I didn't know where I was going. Maybe I was hoping to go to America. But the French humanitarian boats picked us up and soon I was living in the housing projects in Clichy-sous-Bois. Tiny, cramped rooms and a communal bathroom I shared with other refugee men. I worked in a meat-smoking factory, on my feet all day, operating the mixer with my hands. But I am not complaining. No, I am proud of that work. Me, I always have a goal and I am always working. But it was not easy. On my first day, the supervisor took me through the factory. He showed me a big pile of sawdust and asked me to wait next to it, while he went away, returning with a shovel in one hand and lots of sacks in the other. He just pointed to the pile and said something in French that I did not understand. Of course, I guessed that he wanted me to shovel the sawdust and fill the sacks. After hours of labour, my whole body was wet with sweat, as if I had been working under a shower. My glasses had fogged with the steam.

I came home that first day, and thought about my life. I looked in the mirror and I saw such an ugly face, and dark yellow skin. I did not even recognise myself. I scratched my cheek and then saw black under my fingernails. I scratched everywhere and it was black—my body was sweating black, like dirt. I thought to myself, *How can I touch a woman like this*? I thought about my loneliness and tears flowed down my face. I had to lock myself in the toilet to hide from the other men. I promised myself that I would work and work to get out of my horrible situation. I saved money to buy crocodile logo shirts and a ticket to Vietnam, and I went back to find a Vietnamese woman.

I wish you could see what my wife was like back then. She was the youngest daughter in a family of four daughters, so shy and small. When I visited the house, she wore a white *áo dài*, like a schoolgirl. She barely said a word. I asked permission to take her to a café. She sat on the back of my scooter, and when I swerved or stopped abruptly, she grabbed onto my waist. She chirped like a bird, every time, it was so sweet. I thought, oh, now I have this pretty winged thing on my back, and I should marry her.

But my wife is so lazy, you know. She came to live with me in Paris and complained about the size of the apartment. Now she complains that I am old. She complains about everything. I made her wash my clothes, but she said that she would not touch my work clothes because my work is disgusting, the barley from the factory sticks to her fingers, and there is always grease on my pants. She thinks it is beneath her, that is the truth. She complains that she does not have her sisters around to talk to. She complains that she does not have new clothes and handbags. I tell her to go and work for money if she wants new clothes. Plenty of Vietnamese women work in hair and nail salons in Paris. So she says to me, *How can you bear to bring the woman you love away from her home and make her clean the feet of white people*? Such a lazy thing. She will not work and she sits at home watching Vietnamese TV shows. She does not even try to learn French. And she grows fat. *The woman you love*, she says. I confide in you, brother, that the thought of love had never crossed my mind.

While we are in Vietnam, she is staying in the Sofitel in Sài Gòn. That's where she makes her sisters visit her. With my money, she buys them bottles of Chanel perfume and crocodile shirts. She buys as much as she can, and if I try to stop her, she says, *You stole my life!* She says it all the time. *You stole my life!* What a failure am I, to have stolen something of no value.

What's the matter? No, I am not drunk. I am sure you are not happy with your life either. I know you. Look at this godforsaken land. Men like us, we are always dreaming, always dreaming. There is always some place we are heading for, isn't there, or there would be no sense in suffering for it. At the end of the war, Vietnam was such a sad and ruined country, like somebody's plaything. I thought to myself, *I will go to a country where the people are rich and powerful and I will learn their ways*. On the refugee boat, I was lying beside a soldier whose leg was infected with gangrene, so I tried not to breathe and I made a promise to myself: *I will succeed, oh, I promise, I promise I will*. It was unbearable for him, and for us all, because his leg was rotting and the rot crept higher up his body every day. Somebody told him that it would soon reach his heart and kill him. We thought about throwing him off the boat, and sometimes he wanted us to, because the pain was so great. But of course it is hard for a man to decide to die, and it is hard to tell a man to die. So in the end, we threw him off the boat.

Will you believe that I did not feel anything? I was not his friend, I did not know his name—those things don't matter on a boat like that. There is a lot of death, and no time to agonise. I arrived in France and life got harder every day. I told myself, this is not it, not yet. I wanted to gain riches from France so that I could return home to Vietnam, where I belonged. I wanted to change, to succeed, so that I could bring it all back home. In my mind, home was a beautiful country, kind women, and good food—food unmatched anywhere, not even by the French. This is where I am stupid, my brother. I dreamed up an ideal home. But what has become of this country, rotten with the Communist gangrene?

On nights like this, I ask myself where I am heading. Have I reached my destination? Is it this yard in a stinking fishing village in the south? Is it Sài Gòn, where my fat wife is emptying my bank account to buy perfume? Is it the apartment in Paris, so small that I hide drunk in the toilet every weekend? Or is it in America with the slaughtered chickens? That is the fate of the immigrant: always the dumb hope that we are going somewhere. *Somewhere, somewhere*, what a curse the word is, and yet it has infested my flesh. What do *you* want, my brother? Where do you dream to go? Is it somewhere with beaches, a big new house? Are there skyscrapers in the background and neon signs? How beautiful is the woman? Tell me, how soft is her hair and how does she hold you when you are worried?

But you must be sick of me. I have been such a terrible host, carrying on all this time about my tedious story. You must hate me. And how do I feel about you? I don't know, brother. I still cannot tell if you will rob me or not, you have been so mysterious and quiet. And here I am, I have talked myself into a drunken stupor. I am weak and you must do what you will, that is how it is. Perhaps it is not so bad, is it? Perhaps it is better that you want something of mine and it will be no different afterwards, except that you will have the things instead of me. If I could just have one request, it is that, if you rob me, if you take my shirt and my phone and my money, please take my wife too. Be thorough. Take my passport. The French will not be able to tell us apart and it will be easy for you to live my life because I have just told you how. Now my head is heavy and aches for the net of the hammock. Nothing will be better than to sink into it. I will wake in the morning with no clothes on, my mouth crusted with squid and saliva and my skin red from this fire. Unless you incinerate me in it, and those sap trees nearby melt down to rivers of glue and cover the whole village in black smoke. What a pair we make, you and me, brother, two robbers in the night.

Black Beans and Wine

I was dating a new guy. He was on my mind as I stirred a
saucepan of black beans and water in my little kitchen in
Arlington County. I had said something terrible to him. The
white eyes of the beans were magnified beneath the water and
filled me with sudden paranoia. I turned down the heat and
let the pot simmer.

For our first date, Sean had taken me to an Italian restaurant in DC, where my vegetables were puréed and squeezed
out into flowers around my plate. I couldn't tell what they
were, maybe a blend of squash, peas and Brussel sprouts,
whipped into a cool blue cream. What would he think if he saw

me picking at a week-old rotisserie chicken or manhandling a jumbo-sized bag of frozen peas from Capitol Supermarket?

Sean said I smelt of madeleines. I'd been testing a new mix of essential oils: four parts orange zest, one part lemon, one part vanilla, and a touch of lavender. Sean told me how, on his way to high school in New Haven, he used to pass a French patisserie where they sold orange-peel madeleines in white boxes with gold lettering. The day after our first date, he sent a box from the Georgetown Bakery to my workplace. Two golden discs nestled in blue tissue paper and a simple card: 'Areej.' I assumed somebody at a stationery shop had written my name, but later Sean told me he did it himself. His handwriting was exquisite. I ate the madeleines on the train home.

I had a lot to think about as I watched the water bubble. Did I have any tomatoes left? I had been thinking about tomatoes all day. Yesterday at work, Guillermo, the new intern, showed me Neruda's 'Oda al Tomate' and in the evening, I ran around the Wakefield High School track in Arlington, thinking about the tomato juices in the poem, cold and fresh, *la totalidad de su frescura*, and imagining lying down on the conference room floor with Guillermo next to the watercooler that bubbled like a forest stream. After the run, I got ready to go to Sean's.

The beans were overcooked; I could smell it in the smoke from the pot. But when I tasted them, I decided that the smokiness worked with the flavour, and the crispy edges were a nice texture.

I balanced the pot on the arm of the couch, where the faux leather was already cracking and ripped. I wondered where

Sean was now. Probably still at the Dupont Circle bar since happy hour, rubbing a sheen of orange Buffalo wing sauce onto his phone screen. I had told him that I was busy tonight, that I had promised to Skype my dad.

'Send him my regards,' Sean had said as I was leaving his apartment this morning. I don't know if anybody has ever sent Dad their regards before. Certainly not a senator's staff assistant.

I sniffed as I shook out my hair from its bun: it reeked of garlic. When I worked part-time at Dad's takeout shop in Sixteen Mile Stand, Ohio, my hair always smelled of garlic, from the garlic-batter shrimp curry.

Dad took everything he could from Grandma's traditional Punjabi kitchen and deep-fried it in buttermilk batter. Even the rice was tossed in oil, cloves and chicken salt.

'You know what this is, Areej?' Dad used to say, pumping oil out of a plastic canister. 'This is *fusion* Pakistani-American food. You should take notes.'

His accent dragged down the *u* in 'fusion', adding four more beats to the word, like a handful of garam masala tossed into a bowl of cornflakes. I laughed and did take notes on how to avoid his accent. In DC, 'fusion' was pronounced with the curt, funnelled *u* and the dishes were deconstructed on long rectangular plates, with slices of pickled ginger on the side.

Send him my regards... Sean looked at me in the same earnest way he did whenever he asked me why I was laughing. He asked it all the time. The first few times, I said, very sweetly, 'At you, you knob.'

This morning, as he was eating me out, he asked again. I was laughing because he was stroking my legs. I was ticklish and I screamed, 'At you, you fuck!' He stopped and looked at me. I just wanted to finish. He went back down and stroked the length of my thighs to my calves, where his fingers encircled my limbs. I wanted to thrash from the feeling of his cool tongue inside me, but he had me pinned. He stroked the nook under my right knee, pressing deeper and deeper as I came, laughing and screaming. As he leaned up to kiss me, I tasted sourness on his lips and decided to be kind to him.

Afterwards, we were sitting on the lawn of the Washington Monument, where the Navy Band Northeast was playing Prokofiev badly. He took my hand.

'You're so beautiful,' he said.

I looked up and was shocked at how unfamiliar his face seemed. His bright blue eyes, the hue of blue sports drinks, were so concerned (*What are you thinking? Are you having a good time?*). I lifted my hand to close his eyelids, but stopped myself just in time.

'What?' he whispered.

I rested my hand on his cheek.

'What,' he said again, even more softly.

So I said:

'I love you.' I laughed, and went home to cook the black beans.

I woke up later that night with my face in the cracked leather and my breath smelling like garlic. I had fallen asleep with *Breaking Bad* still playing on my laptop. My housemate, Payal, back from parent-teacher night at Wakefield High School, where she was a careers counsellor, was swearing loudly in the bathroom. I got up to investigate and found her wrestling with the large bucket I had left by the sink. I helped her pull the bucket upright and the red liquid sloshed over the floor.

'What the fuck is this, did you period into this thing?' said Payal.

'No, fuck you. It's the wine I'm making. It's not supposed to be opened for another month,' I said.

I squatted over the bucket, shoving the thick lid back into its seal, even though I knew it was too late.

'You could have warned me. I'm not cleaning it up,' said Payal.

She had taken off her underwear and was stepping into the bathtub. 'Fucking wine in the bathroom,' she muttered.

I mopped up the wine with an old shirt from the laundry basket, but most of the spill had already seeped into the exposed concrete where the tiles were cracked.

As I bent over, my head began to spin. Heaving, I leaned into the toilet bowl, globs of spit dangling from my tongue. Payal stood under the shower, watching me.

'Why do you drink when it makes you such a fucking mess?'

'I didn't drink that much.'

'Then what's wrong?'

'Nothing, just feel kinda weird.'

'Tell me and I'll help you clean this up.'

'Don't treat me like one of your kids.'

'Tell me in one word.'

'What? I don't know the word,' I said.

'Think harder.'

'Payal, I don't know.'

'What's it feel like?'

'Disgust.'

'What are you disgusted with? Sean?' she asked.

'You said one word.'

Her shoulders drooped. 'Okay... Have you had dinner? I was gonna make a cheesy-potato bake.'

I was so hungry. We went into the kitchen, where I watched her peel eight potatoes and slice them into thin disks. I felt better as she lined up the disks in a tray and poured in a milk-butter-mozzarella batter.

The next evening, at a ball in the Library of Congress, Sean introduced me to his boss.

'Areej. Is that Arabic?' she asked.

'I'm Pakistani.'

'I mean, what language do you speak?'

'English,' I said, enjoying the panic on Sean's face.

Everyone Sean introduced me to that night had asked where I was from. I took a passing hors d'oeuvre and bit into the hard bread topped with chopped tomato, herbs and black vinaigrette, which dribbled to the sides of my mouth and stung. I washed it down with champagne.

'Your people have such a rich and interesting culture,' she said, and turned to Sean. 'She's so beautiful.'

'She's an Institutional Philanthropy and Partnerships Officer at the International Rescue Committee,' he said.

Sean had also been reciting that line all night. In a city where everyone spoke in acronyms, I couldn't help thinking that Sean was spelling out my title, and the IRC, in an attempt to justify my presence there. Some people feigned interest, but an NGO couldn't make them pay attention the way a political office did. His boss didn't acknowledge it.

'Well, I hope you enjoy your evening here…' She smiled. She had already forgotten my name. 'It's a gorgeous space.'

'It really is,' Sean said amiably, and looked up at the ceiling as though just inspired to take it in.

The Great Hall in the Library of Congress was lined with tall Roman columns, arching into the murals of its marbled ceiling. We were standing by the side of the grand staircase, where a plaster bust of a historical figure I didn't recognise was set into the wall. (Washington? Jefferson? Adams?) Positioned at eye level, his head on a slight angle and his brow furrowed, he appraised the guests in the room.

'We're lucky to be here,' said Sean's boss.

I leaned across Sean to stop a passing waitress, took another flute of champagne off her tray and drank most of it in one gulp.

As his boss left, Sean leaned in to kiss me. I knew my breath was rancid from the vinaigrette, but I muttered into his mouth:

'If you don't take me home right now, I'll break up with you.'

I wanted to say more. I was drunk. I wanted to keep speaking, just so he could smell the sourness.

The vinegar made me think of all the smells I hated, especially the curries that used to stain my plastic lunchboxes, stick to my clothes and follow me down Montgomery Road from school to Dad's takeaway shop. I spent evenings by the sink scrubbing my lunchboxes and then, later on, scrubbing at my armpits.

It was too early to tell Sean about my childhood. I could tell he assumed my upbringing was similar to his, because that was all he knew, from suburban New Haven to Harvard for college, to a career at the US Capitol. He made me feel as if I was constantly pretending to fit into his world: the way he ate, the way he talked about travel, about college, and the casual references to family money that every civil servant and NGO employee in DC made. The assumptions everyone held were so strong that I had to either make dramatic confessions to correct them or play along. It was easier to play along. I wasn't ready to talk yet, and I couldn't stand to see Sean's reaction to any of it.

The first time I tried to leave home at sixteen, I came back two months later. I was at my skinniest and my friend Sarah was sick of me.

'You look disgusting,' Dad said, when he opened the door. I had on the old tracksuit I used to wear at home.

Behind the flyscreen, Mom stifled a moan. She started sobbing when Dad led me to the living room and gestured to the couch.

'You have worried your mother sick.'

I fingered the loose skin around my wrists.

'You think we don't know where you've been?'

'I don't know.'

'Your mother wants to die because her only daughter is sleeping like a dog on the street.'

'Then why doesn't she tell me?'

Mom stood over by the window. She didn't know what we were saying. I could still understand Punjabi but hadn't spoken it since starting high school. Dad's English was even shakier in his anger, as if he was trying to play some character he had seen on TV. His arms were stiff and jerking, as though ready to strike me. But I knew he wouldn't. He sat on the other end of the couch, a small man in a green-and-white-striped polo shirt, hunched over, keening on his living room couch.

He had already disowned me when I walked out, even though he came knocking on Sarah's door, begging me to come back. I told him then that he had lost me long ago, when he let his customers leer at me, saying nothing but 'please' and 'thank you' to them.

But it sounded weak when I said it to his face. I wanted to tell him more: about Uncle Saif stroking circles on my thigh, where my jeans were ripped, as I sat in the back of the Land Rover during the two-hour drive to the family holidays at Lake Erie. About the big weddings, when the men drank too much and I had to pose for photos, feeling hands on my waist where the sari left my skin exposed. About the way my forty-seven-year-old Pakistani tutor, a family friend, called me beautiful, caressing my arms and shoulders encouragingly while he stared at my breasts, then took home Mom's pakoras after our sessions. About Sachith, Dad's long-time employee at the takeout shop, who first had sex with me when I was fifteen and he was twenty-eight, and didn't stop until he got married and invited our whole family to his wedding. But I was afraid it wouldn't be enough. I wanted Dad to feel my disgust, but I knew I could never convince him of it.

Standing outside Sarah's house, he curled his upper lip and said, 'You are so full of hate.'

Sean didn't say much on the way home from the ball.

I watched his profile as he drove. His collar was so perfectly straight. I thought about the day we went to Barney's to buy him new shirts, and how nice it felt that he liked everything I picked out for him.

He drew a deep breath as he slid the car into my driveway and turned off the engine. All of a sudden, I was desperately afraid that he was angry. But he turned to me and said:

'You know you can tell me anything.'

Had he guessed what I had been thinking? Suddenly, it no longer felt fun to indulge whatever fantasies he had about me.

Inside, he ducked as he stepped down from the living room to the kitchen, where the ceiling was low. I glanced at his leather shoes. He hadn't noticed that we left shoes at the front doorstep.

'What's that smell?' he asked.

I stared at him, my back to the sink.

'What's wrong?' he asked, sounding frustrated.

'It's the wine I'm making,' I said.

I was on the brink of tears.

I first started making wine three years ago when I was unemployed after graduation, and staying in Aurora, Ohio with Aunt Laksha and her family. They had a small house with dirty white walls, sitting on a bed of weeds. I made wine in the barn, in between sending off resumes. My cousins Noor and Eric, who were five and six, thought it was fantastic. They used to visit me in the barn and I pretended I was a witch concocting potions to turn children into mushrooms. They ran off screaming, 'Areej is a witch! Areej is a witch!'

One night, Aunt Laksha sat me down at the kitchen table.

'I worry about you. You are a very lucky girl, you know. You have good family and you are so beautiful. Look, what man would not want this?' She patted my C-cup breasts. 'What is wrong with you?'

'Nothing's wrong with me.'

'You are not normal.'

'That's just because I'm drunk, Auntie.'

Her eyes filled with tears.

'How shall I answer to your father!' She wrung her gold bracelets. 'Oh, Allah help me!' she cried.

I was drinking a lot because there was no one to try my wine and nothing else to do in Aurora. After the talk with Aunt Laksha, I went for a long walk around the neighbourhood. I would later visit many other American cities, but no other where the streets were level with the footpath and there were no curbs. In Aunt Laksha's neighbourhood, the ground was flat for miles in every direction. Powdery-white streets blended into off-white driveways, cut by polite squares of grass that had been watered a pale green.

I bought a bunch of hibiscus at the florist and took it back to boil in the barn. After dissolving the flower water with sugar and a bit of acid, I let it cool before plunging my hands in the tub to squeeze the flowers for more flavour. It took me hours and my arms were stained hibiscus-red up to my elbows. Noor and Eric came in after dinner.

'Mommy is mad you didn't come to dinner,' said Eric.

'Tell Auntie I've already eaten,' I said.

'But she made kofta,' said Noor.

'Hey, come here,' I said.

I dried my hands on my shirt and stuck hibiscus flowers behind their ears. I had saved two of the prettiest ones for them.

'This is a very strong flower and if you wear it close to your head, it will grow beautiful thoughts inside you,' I said.

'You smell like a goddess,' said Noor.

'I thought I was a witch.'

The whole barn smelt of flowers and sugar; I hadn't added the yeast yet. Noor and Eric stayed playing with the wet hibiscus mulch until bedtime. It was the last time I felt beautiful.

Sean's jaw tensed as though he was going to yell at me. I thought, wildly, that the spell had broken.

'You make *wine*?' said Sean.

'Yeah.'

'Well then I have to try some,' he said, his tone so forced and positive it disgusted me.

I went to the bathroom to fill a jug with the red liquid. Back in the living room, I poured two glasses and swilled them in Sean's face. I drank mine in one gulp. It was awful. The flowers were bitter, so tart from the yeast that my mouth ached. I poured another glass and it sank hot and sour to my stomach.

I hated the way Sean was looking at me. I hated that he wouldn't admit how awful the wine was. He drank his glass and didn't say another word. I started undoing his belt and he gripped my arm, as though in shock. I laughed into his face, my breath full of yeast, until his grip loosened and he let me pull down his pants. I turned around and we had sex against the kitchen sink.

I woke at dawn, my head pounding. Sean was still asleep on the couch. I was horrified to find the bucket half-empty and worried that I had made him sick. I went out into the garden, startled to find the April morning so bright. A pale yellow glow seemed to emanate from the plants, and I lay on the grass to warm my skin. I noticed a bud of orange above my head and plucked off the first tomato of the year, crying for all the things I had made and ruined.

Mekong Love

It was on the night of the matchmaking ceremony that Comma received her first threat. She was alone when she found it, on her evening trip to fetch water from the family well. Everyone on this side of the River Ba Rại, a small distributary of the Mekong Delta, knew that Comma was the one who did the Trương family's final water run of the day. It could not have been more clear that the threat was meant for Comma, and Comma only. The well was out by the family graves; no one else had any business being there after sunset.

Sitting on the rim of the Trươngs' well, the threat was a careful and monstrous curation of items. It was sitting on the mouth: a fistful of bloody, matted chicken feathers, a hand-written note stained with blood, presumably the chicken's, and a black lock of human hair, all lying neatly atop a banana leaf. Though Comma did not know what the note said, she had no doubt of the maliciousness of the display. She stifled a scream when she saw it in the waning evening light, not so much because it frightened her, but in this ugly arrangement she could read the mad, jealous passions of Vietnam's deep south.

Cai Lậy, a rural province in Vietnam's Mekong Delta, was right in the centre of the dragon's belly. Southerners called the Mekong the Nine Dragons River: when it snaked and wriggled down the country's length, it split into nine branches before spilling into the sea at each dragon's mouth. Fat, gaudy durians grew out of skinny trees along the riverbanks, weighing down the branches so that they were closer to the river-dragons wanting a taste. Then there were the soursops, papayas, mangoes, dragonfruits and jackfruits, which grew so quickly that sons and daughters had to cut them down daily, lest the rotting fruits attract flies.

The fruit here was sweeter and more pungent than fruit found anywhere else in Vietnam, and the people who ate it had insatiable appetites. Perhaps the miraculous fertility of the land, the richness of its tastes, its beauty, led them to trust nature and surrender themselves to it. Passions were indulged, because such things were fickle. Children were often lost to nature. Newborns were neither named, spoken of nor seen by anyone who did not live in the home, because nature could reclaim babies as wantonly as it created them. Children were given ugly names, after uninspiring objects, so they could be hidden from powerful spirits that roamed the country for precious things.

The Mekong Delta was an important part of how the southerners saw themselves as different from the rest of Vietnam. Northerners, with their stiff, precise accents and cold mountains bordering China, had the Red River, thick and brown as old blood, carrying down into Vietnam the cold and greed (and, once the civil war had come, communism) of neighbouring China, an ancient enemy of Vietnam. The middle of the country, once the home of Vietnam's monarchy, had the Perfume River, named for the gentle fragrance of flower orchards that wafted down the water. The romance of the Perfume River, often pictured at a soft-pink sunset, evoked nostalgia for Vietnam's bygone grandeur and elegance. Southerners will attest to the beauty of the Perfume River (although few would see it in their lifetimes), but the Mekong would always be the most real: fertile, heady and lush. Its people were the most outspoken, the most free, and ate the best food.

Comma, however, was a remarkably cool-headed daughter of the Mekong. After staring at the monstrous items for a moment, she used one foot to gouge a hole in the dirt by the side of the well, into which she tipped the chicken feathers and the hair—long, shiny, and black, unmistakably the hair of a young Vietnamese woman. She covered the hole so that none of her family members would be frightened if they came by the well the next day. The Trương liked to keep things neat and clean; it would be unusual to have bloodied chicken feathers lying anywhere on their land. Especially not by the ancestors' graves, Comma thought. She rinsed the reusable banana leaf and slipped it into the pocket of her pants, along with the handwritten note. In the morning, she would try to find someone to read the note. She then loaded up with water and set off home.

Only at night, in the room she shared with her four sisters, and after she was sure they were asleep, did Comma let herself think about the threat. She had no doubt it concerned Slip. Slip, whom she was still too shy to think about. Slip was the nineteen-year-old eldest son of the Nguyễn family, who lived seven houses down from the Trương. Ever since he'd turned sixteen, everybody in Cai Lậy had known that he would be one of their province's most sought-after bachelors. He had been handsome even then: tall, large eyes, thick black hair and a strong jaw. But, of course, it was not only his looks. The parents in Cai Lậy liked him because he was a responsible, obedient son. He was never a problem for the family; he never drank alcohol or took girls behind bushes (as far as they knew); he was a beloved brother and was said to be very close to his mother, who was often sickly.

But Comma had never spoken with him. Until earlier that day, she had never even looked directly at him. At the matchmaking ceremony, only Slip's and Comma's parents had spoken. She and her younger sister Apostrophe had served rambutans and Oolong tea, which the Nguyễn had brought as formal gifts. Usually, this first step of matchmaking was only for the parents to get to know each other, after which the families would make a decision about whether to proceed or not. But this meeting was different. The Nguyễns and the Trương had known and respected each other for a long time. Slip's mother had visited the Trương' home from time to time and seen how well Comma worked at her chores and took care of her seven younger siblings. It would be too rude for either party to withdraw from the match now, after having agreed to this first meeting. Slip was surely going to become Comma's husband.

All eyes in the room were on Comma and Slip when she approached him for the first time, to serve his tea. Comma did not like the attention, but knew she had to be obliging. After he had accepted the cup, she allowed herself to glance at him. He was staring fixedly at his cup. She noticed the straight line of his lips. Slightly wider lips than usual, she thought, and her cheeks flushed with the outrageous idea that she might kiss those lips one day. Comma bowed her head. The adults in the room, satisfied with the couple's first encounter, turned back to their conversations with each other.

When Comma first knew her parents were making the match, she was not entirely pleased. Slip was too much of a celebrity for Comma's taste. She wanted a more modest match. Beyond that, she had not given much thought to her arranged marriage, except that she would be sad to leave her siblings and wanted to live as close to her family as possible. Besides, Comma knew she was no particular beauty, average in most aspects, except for her eyes, which were a strikingly darker brown than one would expect in this part of her country. The most beautiful daughter in the family was Apostrophe, the second daughter, but no respectable family would propose a match with the second daughter while the eldest daughter was still unmarried.

And there she was, already receiving threats about the match. Lying on the bamboo mat, Comma listened anxiously to the sounds outside. The chickens were agitated, scuttling on the packed dirt and sometimes scraping their feet against the house, as though desperate to enter. There was a restless rustling noise. If it was leaves, it meant her little sister Dash had not swept the yard properly, and poor Dash had been told off enough times by their parents for being sloppy with her chores. If it was snakes, there would be so much work to do to rid the property of vermin. The occasional revving of a moped engine or the squeak of a bike came from the main road at the front of their house along the River Ba Rại. Comma worried that it would be the Vũ father coming home after a heavy night of drinking. The fourteen-year-old Vũ boy, Cường, had confided in Comma that sometimes his father hit his mother; Cường and his mother would sleep outside in the hammocks in the yard, too afraid to go back into the house. Sometimes at night, she thought she could hear them crying. How many people in Cai Lậy cried in the night, Comma wondered. That worried her too.

Comma listened, knowing that somewhere out there was a person coming after her, someone trying to wage war on her.

64

For the first time since learning about the match with Slip, Comma felt a fire light up inside her.

▧

Everyone on this side of the River Ba Rại knew that Slip was the only boy who cut grass at the back of the Nguyễn property. He did this infrequently, because no one ever went out the back of the property. But Mr Nguyễn liked things to be tidy, and sometimes he could sell the grass to buffalo owners. Slip liked to cut grass in the evening, after finishing his chores.

On the evening of the first matchmaking ceremony at the Trương, he decided to go out to check it. He had neglected it lately, perhaps because of the matchmaking. His mother had fretted so much over what to bring to the Trương that day, and yet it hardly seemed to matter. Comma's parents did not eat the rambutan.

Cutting the grass would give him some time away from his family, especially his mother, who scrutinised every reaction of his to the matchmaking. He had been careful not to show any particular pleasure or displeasure about the match. His parents might read too much into it and think that he was criticising their choice. It was a full-moon night—he didn't really know what to make of that—and it was a cool night, which made the work easier.

Once he had finished, Slip tied up the cut grass with some rope he had strung round his waist and slung the bundles over his shoulder. The grass was heavy and his footprints along the soft dirt road were deeper than usual. He was looking forward to eating more of the bamboo and mushrooms that his mother had made for dinner. He had been getting hungrier and hungrier lately, and his mother now left a bowl of rice and an extra serving of food under a net for him in the kitchen every night. Maybe after eating, he would sit by the river with his little brother Fall, to see if they could catch some fish before bed.

Shortly after Slip had gone home, a young woman came along the narrow path over the pond between the Nguyễns' and the Lýs' properties. She waded through the field, breathing in the scent of grass still fresh from the cutting. She found the footprints Slip had left only half an hour ago and lay down on her side next to the outlines of his feet, tenderly pressing her fingers into the dirt that had been tamped by Slip's steps.

She lay like this for some time, crying softly. She thought about the Nguyễn family not far away, who must be going to sleep now. And she thought about the romance of the full-moon night. The cicadas were telling each other about her and she wanted to explain her great love to them—and to the starry sky and the fresh grass blades. But soon she felt goosebumps on her arms and then she was shivering in the cool night air. Reluctantly, she got up and squatted by the footprints. She took a banana leaf from her pocket and gently scooped the dirt of a footprint onto the leaf. She folded the leaf, tied it up with string like a New Year sticky-rice cake, and made her way home.

The only member of Comma's family who could read was her little sister, ten-year-old Paragraph. Assuming the note would be malicious, Comma couldn't ask Paragraph to read it. She knew the Cai Lậy pharmacist could read; Miss Salt was also the Trương' go-to letter-writer. But Miss Salt would tell Comma's parents about the note and Comma didn't know if she was ready for that.

Comma decided to ask Apostrophe, the second-eldest sister, for advice. That morning, as Comma and Apostrophe loaded their bikes with the baskets of catfish, guava, water spinach and jars of cured lemon, Comma whispered to her about the note.

'You have to let me see it!' Apostrophe cried, her eyes wide.

Comma fished the note out of the pocket of her brown *bà ba* pants, the modest shirt-and-pant ensemble of the southern woman, with two cuts up the side of the shirt for easy movement.

'You carried it *with you*? Are you mad? It could be cursed!' Apostrophe's voice rose even higher. 'It *is* a curse.'

'I couldn't leave it anywhere, could I, where somebody else could find it,' Comma said, softly, still afraid someone could hear them. She was glad that she had not told Apostrophe about the chicken feathers and the hair. 'Besides, there are no such things as curses.'

'No such thing! No such *thing*!'

Apostrophe kept exclaiming as they rode to the Cai Lậy floating market. It was a small market, thirty-odd boats per morning—nowhere near as big as the Cái Bè floating market, where hundreds of boats arrived every day, but the Trườngs had regular customers, especially for their water spinach. The catfish didn't do as well. The Trương boys were digging another pond on the property that very day, in order to breed more fish to sell. On the steep riverbank by their canoe, Apostrophe held the two bikes in place while Comma tied their baskets onto the canoe.

Comma's fingers were calloused and her arms were taut from working ropes. She had learnt about knots from fishermen at the floating market. In fact, she had learnt from five different fishermen before choosing her favourite, and then taught the skill to her little brothers. Now, she deftly selected a top strand of rope, pushed it gently out of its loop, flipped it out of another loop, and the intricate knot unfurled smoothly between her fingers. She wrapped it around a bucket they kept on the canoe for gutting and cleaning the fish. Once Apostrophe was safely aboard, she pushed the canoe into the water before jumping into it herself.

By the time the canoe made its way down the small stream and approached the thoroughfare of the floating market, Apostrophe had concocted a plan.

'Uncle Cup's thirteen-year-old son Table should be able to read your note,' said Apostrophe.

'Table, isn't he—'

'I know. He can't really speak, but he's not dumb. He can read. He's just…' Apostrophe arched an eyebrow. 'Shy.'

'But you can't go straight to Uncle Cup's boat. He would tell everyone,' said Comma.

'That's why I'm going to get Auntie Pillar's son Leg to pass it on to Table. It's a bit early in the week, but we can pass by Auntie Pillar's boat for condiments. There must be something you can tell her that we've run out of. Fish sauce? And while you're making the trade, I'll give Leg the note and tell him what to do,' said Apostrophe.

'But how will we—'

'Get the note back? Leg will ask his mother if he can help us unload our goods off the boat at the end of the morning— he will give the note back to us then,' Apostrophe continued.

'Leg would do it?'

'He'll do it,' Apostrophe smiled, and two dimples emerged in her soft cheeks. 'And he'll keep quiet about it too.'

As Comma paddled, Apostrophe smoothed two evenly parted bundles of hair down the front of her chest and began to plait the strands. She liked to arrive at the market with her hair down, to show how smooth and elegant she could keep it, like a Sài Gòn schoolgirl, before doing it up like a Cai Lậy marketwoman. And she knew that people liked to watch as her fingers moved delicately and precisely between the black locks that flashed in the morning sun.

Comma continued working the paddles, glad to have the grip of them in her palms and to feel the thickness of the Mekong water beneath her. As the sun rose, the market people floated into view. Canoe after canoe, laden with piles of vegetables and fruits, and meat and fish freshly killed and gleaming in buckets of ice, drifted in and lined up along the river. The growers stood guarding their goods, each person's silhouette cut out on the horizon by the *nón lá*, the conical, palm-leaf Vietnamese hat. Comma and Apostrophe's hats were fastened to their chins with a pink polka-dotted strip of fabric that Apostrophe had fashioned. The Mekong water was waking up to the call of its people, and soon the burble of neighbourly greetings, bartering, gossip, fights and laughter settled in.

In this exuberant atmosphere, Apostrophe fitted in perfectly. She was *lanh*, quick-witted and chatty, praise fondly given to southern women who were well liked. Comma's contrasting reserve would usually raise suspicion, but the people in Cai Lậy had come to understand that she was kind and dutiful, a generous marketwoman and the eldest daughter who had raised most of her younger siblings. Some gossiped that Comma's introverted manner was a reflection of a dull spirit, from being forced to shoulder responsibilities too quickly. Things would be better when she married, they said. That would cheer her up.

Comma and Apostrophe made their way down the river. They traded water spinach for bittermelon, cured lemon for sugarcane, guava for mangoes, and sold the occasional fat, whiskered catfish. Soon enough they reached Auntie Pillar.

'Heavens, Auntie Pillar, have your pickled radishes have sold out already?' Apostrophe exclaimed as Comma manoeuvred their canoe beside Auntie Pillar's.

'Everyone knows I make the most flavourful pickled radishes in Cai Lậy. If only you had come earlier, instead of hanging about by that Auntie Rain's boat. Tell me the truth, Apostrophe, were you buying pickled radishes from her?'

'Heavens, no! How my mother would beat me if she knew I was bringing anything but the best pickled radishes home. Please tell me you can make something work for me today, Auntie Pillar.' Apostrophe pouted happily.

'Good thing I knew you are a sensible young girl—I saved you this jar.' Auntie Pillar fished a small jar out from under a pile of fresh white radish and handed it to Apostrophe.

'Three thousand,' Auntie Pillar said to Comma, who had the three notes ready to pass over. 'And is business going well, Comma?'

'As well as we can hope for,' Comma said politely.

'We're not having much luck with the catfish this morning,' Apostrophe said with a sigh.

'A lot of competition for catfish lately, isn't there?' said Auntie Pillar.

'We don't mean to complain,' said Apostrophe. 'But all the catfish we don't sell here has to go to the land market. It's far away and Comma and I struggle with the heavy load.'

'You know, I hardly have anything left to sell,' said Auntie Pillar. 'I don't really need Leg to help me bring things home. Maybe I can send him to help you girls? Hey—*Leg!*'

A twelve-year-old boy bounded across four adjoining boats to reach his mother's side. He froze when he saw that his mother was talking to Apostrophe, who smiled brilliantly at him.

'Leg, you'll be helping these girls bring their catfish to the land market at the end of the morning,' said Auntie Pillar.

'Hey, come here, Leg, let me see how tall and strong you've

grown! Are you are up to the task?' said Apostrophe. She waved him over and offered him a guava out of the basket at the end of their boat.

'Say, do you have any fish sauce left, Auntie?' Comma said quickly.

As Auntie Pillar packaged the fish sauce, scooping it from a bucket into a clear plastic bag, Comma glanced at Apostrophe and Leg. The boy had just slipped the piece of paper into his pocket.

Anxious to please one of the beauties of Cai Lậy, he bounced from boat to boat up the floating market to Uncle Cup's durian boat, found out that his son Table was home for the day, went back up the riverbank and rode his bike down to the Lê house to find Table, asked Table to read the message out and repeat it three times over so that he could memorise it for Apostrophe.

At the end of the morning, when Comma and Apostrophe pulled up to their part of the riverbank, Leg was waiting. Apostrophe ran up the bank to meet him. She leaned her cheek to his lips to hear the message that he had brought for her from the other end of Cai Lậy. Comma watched on anxiously beside the canoe, her feet still in the water. She saw Apostrophe's eyes grow wide.

IF YOU MARRY HIM I WILL KILL YOU.

Comma received three more threats before the wedding. The next one was waiting for her one Sunday morning in the curing shed behind the house. Another of Comma's chores was to organise the storage of the Trường' jars of lemon, kumquat, salted fish and radishes. In the middle of the dirt floor was a freshly slain chicken, slashed at the throat, a pool of dried blood beneath it. One of its wings was twisted grotesquely where another handwritten note had been clipped.

It was still too early for her family to be up, so Comma left the ghastly display in the curing shed and dashed outside to count the chickens. Her heart raced. One was missing. She ran back into the shed and stared at the dead chicken. She picked it up, swept her sandals several times over the dirt floor to smooth it down, and took the dead bird to the outdoor kitchen. She was certain that her enemy would not have said the prayer, *Nam mô A Di Đà Phật*, to the chicken before cutting its throat. Comma had taught her brothers and sisters to say the prayer before killing any of the family chickens, to acknowledge that a life was being sacrificed for the family's nourishment. It vexed her that this one had died for nothing but revenge.

In the kitchen, Comma plucked out the chicken's feathers, cleaned it and began cooking. She started a broth with the bones and cooked the meat for the family lunch: green papaya salad with shredded chicken.

On Monday morning, once again, word was sent along the river through Apostrophe, Leg and Table, and came back down to Comma.

DON'T YOU BELIEVE I WILL KILL YOU, YOU WHORE?

At night, before she fell asleep, Comma was haunted by the scraping of the chicken running in the yard. Someone had come right onto their property, so close to the sleeping family, and taken something that wasn't theirs.

The third threat came the morning after the wedding date was set. While Comma and Apostrophe were riding their bikes to the floating market, Comma reached into the pocket of her *bà ba*. She screamed as she felt needles stabbing her hand. Startled, Apostrophe lost balance and her bike come crashing down, the basket of market goods on top of it. After helping Apostrophe to pull the bike upright again, Comma turned out her pocket.

Along with her handkerchief, a cloth voodoo doll tumbled out. Comma picked it up gingerly. A grotesque face had been painted, smudged, on the doll and three needles were stuck on it, in…

'In the *vagina*,' Apostrophe gasped. There was no note this time.

The sisters stopped their trip in order to burn the voodoo doll. Apostrophe cried as the little cloth doll smouldered.

'There has to be an end to this,' Apostrophe sobbed. 'How many more of these do you think she has out there?'

Comma could not really imagine the stranger who sent her these messages as a real person, a real woman who lived somewhere amongst them in Cai Lậy.

'There's nothing we can do,' said Comma.

'How can you be so *calm*!' Apostrophe's sobs increased. 'Wake up, Comma! This woman is a real danger. She's *crazy*. She wants to *kill you*.'

'I don't think she really would,' murmured Comma.

'What's wrong with you? Why don't you ever feel anything?!' Apostrophe cried.

Comma waited a moment before coming over to hug her sister. She had been asking herself the same question. She had now formally met and exchanged greetings with Slip at the engagement ceremony when she knelt before their parents—and felt nothing. And all she felt now was anxiety that her mother and Apostrophe would not be able to manage the Trương house on their own, and vague concern about how many women had told her she should be excited to marry the most handsome young man in Cai Lậy. It was early days, she told herself. In the meantime, her worry for her family weighed more heavily in her heart than the mysterious woman sending her threats.

When the sisters finally arrived at the market—late for the first time in years—onlookers were surprised by the sight of Apostrophe paddling the canoe, while Comma nursed her right hand.

The fourth threat arrived the day before the wedding. In the middle of the night, someone had poured a shocking amount of blood—it must have been almost a bucketful—all over the pale stone entrance to the Trương house. A chicken's head, only the head, lay in the blood, a note in its beak.

The stench of the blood woke Comma's father from his sleep. Searching the house for the source of the smell, he soon found it at his door.

'What is the meaning of this?' he thundered, waking all nine members of the family.

Tearfully, Comma and Apostrophe told their parents about the previous threats. Apostrophe was still upset by their monstrousness, while Comma was filled with the shame of having kept secrets from her parents.

The four of them were sitting in the formal living room by the family altar. Two of the boys had been sent to clean the blood from their door and the rest of the children were in the girls' bedroom. Their mother had started crying from the moment she heard her husband's raised voice and was now sitting with Apostrophe, clinging to her as they both sobbed.

Comma's father looked at her carefully.

'What do you want to do about this?' he asked.

Comma was startled. Though he often relied on her to take care of things around the house, she assumed that it would be his decision on how to handle the threats. She had not expected him to consult her. His expression was weary. She realised that he had no idea what to do.

'I don't know,' she said.

They had already ruled out sending for Table or anyone else to read the note. They could not risk the community finding out about the threat. It did not really matter what the note said anyway. The message was clear.

'Do you want to go ahead with the wedding?' Comma's father asked.

Again, Comma was startled. It would be scandalous to call

off the wedding. Their relationship with the Nguyễns would not survive it, and they would be the source of gossip and derision for years to come: the family who arrogantly, rudely, left the most eligible bachelor of Cai Lậy at the altar. Yet she could tell by her father's manner, by his vulnerability—which unsettled her more than she was prepared for—that he really would call off the wedding if she wanted to. She glanced at her mother and at Apostrophe, who were staring at her, their eyes shining. And then she felt it—the spark of courage, of passion, that had ignited in her on the night of the first threat.

'Yes,' said Comma. 'Real gold has no fear of fire.'

The night before the wedding, the young woman was back among the grass blades at the back of the Nguyễn property. Was it a coincidence that Slip had chosen this night, of all nights, to come out to this field and cut the grass again? She could not help feeling that he knew she was out there for him. How could he not? She lay down again beside his footprints in the dirt. She picked up some of the dirt from the imprint of his feet and pressed it to her cheek, imagining she could feel the warmth of his skin.

How could he not know, she asked the cicadas and the half moon. She did not believe it was possible to have this much love for someone, and for him not to feel it. Her love must reach him somehow, somewhere in his aura, or in his dreams, giving him the invisible reassurance that he was safe in the world because he was loved. She wondered, agonised, if he knew where this love was coming from ... But how could he know when she could not reveal herself to him?

'It's *me*, Slip, it's me, it's me, it's all mine,' she whispered into the dirt.

Comma and Slip's wedding proceeded smoothly. Slip's popularity and the good reputation of their two families brought what seemed like the entire population of Cai Lậy out onto the main road by the River Ba Rại in the morning. During the first ceremony, the groom and his family came to the bride's house with gifts, to ask the elders of her family for her hand. Led by his father, Slip and his seven groomsmen, each in the deep blue-and-gold men's traditional dress, walked in formal procession to the Trương house, bearing tray after tray of food covered in bright-red cloth.

Next, the groom's procession came back down the same path to the Nguyễn household, this time with Comma, who was swathed in the dazzling lucky red of the bride's *áo dài* dress. The golden *khăn đóng* headpiece held her hair off her face and brought out the startling dark brown of her eyes.

As the wedding party approached the entrance of the Nguyễn house, firecrackers exploded, filling the air with festive smoke. Inside, Comma knelt before the elders of her new family. She was poised and graceful. She lifted the ceremonial china cup on its saucer above her head; there was not the slightest rattle. Slip's mother fastened gold earrings to Comma's earlobes and each set of parents presented a bar of gold to the couple.

The reception was held in the yard by the main Nguyễn

house. There were almost three hundred guests; it was one of the larger weddings in Cai Lậy. All the women in the extended Nguyễn family—some of whom had travelled from neighbouring provinces—had been busy for days with food preparations, mostly fish—fish hotpot and fish summer rolls. The translucent rice paper held a riot of colour: beds of white rice noodles, glistening pink fish flesh, the yellow and orange of diced pineapple and mango, and the different shades of green in the herbs and leaves. There was also the dark, sticky peanut dipping sauce. For dessert, hundreds of bowls were filled with a mixture of red bean, green bean, tapioca and grass jelly, swimming in coconut milk and topped with shaved ice. By sunset, the men were happily drunk, the women chatting in cozy circles, and the children were left free to roam.

At the end of the night, a raucous group of groomsmen and bridesmaids accompanied Comma and Slip to their new home, a small one-room house on the Nguyễn property built for the new couple by Slip, his brothers and his uncles. As their brothers and sisters left, the happy conversation and giggling fading away, Comma and Slip were alone for the first time. They stared around them at their new home.

Comma's brothers had brought over bags of her things, and lined them up neatly in the corner of the house. Not looking at Slip, she knelt down by the bags and busied herself with her toiletries. With her back to Slip, she began to undo the red *áo dài*, unhooking the row of buttons that ran from her neck, down her shoulders to her armpit. She put on silk pants and tied up the strings of her new *yếm*, a silk halter-neck

79

and backless top worn as undergarment. Comma wasn't sure if she should only wear the *yếm* by itself, then decided to put on a jacket as well. She turned and saw that Slip had already changed. She wandered if he had seen her naked back.

While Comma was in the outdoor kitchen behind the house, washing off her make-up, she heard Slip putting a pot on the stove. When she came back inside, he had finished brewing tea and was bringing it over on a tray with two cups.

He placed the tray in the middle the bedspread and sat down on the edge of the bed. Comma sat on the other side. She glanced at him as she took her cup. Were they now going to talk about what happened on a wedding night?

'Are you cold?' Slip asked her.

'No, I'm fine,' Comma replied.

'We were afraid that the thatching of the walls was not tight enough,' said Slip.

'It's a beautiful house,' said Comma. 'Besides, even if there are gaps in the walls, it's nice to have a breeze coming in at night. As long as the roof doesn't leak.'

'Yes, the roof is well-layered. It won't leak,' said Slip.

They sipped on their tea. Comma recognised the floral fragrance, but could not put her finger on the name of the flower.

'Are you tired?' asked Slip.

'Yes, a bit,' she said. 'Are you?'

'Yes, I think so,' he said. He took a few more sips of tea. 'Did you have a good day?'

'I did. Did you?'

'Yes,' said Slip. His voice trailed with an unfinished thought. Comma waited patiently for him to continue. 'Shall we go to sleep?'

Comma froze, wondering if he meant what she thought he could mean, and what would come next.

'We can talk more tomorrow morning,' he said.

He put the tea tray away, came back to the bedroom, lifted the blanket and lay down. Comma remained seated, imagining all the different ways in which he might start touching her, feeling unprepared for each of them. But when she eventually turned around to look at him, his eyes were closed.

In the moonlight filtering through the little room, Comma stared at her husband. He really was very handsome. She thought of all the women who would want to gaze at him as she was now: the mysterious woman who did not kill her after all, for example. Yet in his sleep, Slip's beauty seemed something private. Was his strong jaw clenched? And were his wide lips, firmly closed, shutting her out? Comma wondered. She kept looking at him, waiting. Surely he was not already asleep. After all, it was their wedding night. But he did not move and eventually she lifted the blanket and lay down. Although the bed was small, there was a surprising amount of space between them, enough for the blanket to lie flat.

Still Comma waited. She was too tense and bewildered to sleep. She hoped he would reach for her at some point, but after what felt like hours, she noticed that his breathing was louder and more rhythmic. He really was asleep. She closed her eyes. Even were it not for Slip's behaviour, it would have been hard for Comma to sleep. All the sounds of the night were different. They were closer to the river here and she could hear the water lapping against the bank. The cicadas sung at a different pitch and rhythm. She thought she could hear the Nguyễns' buffaloes snoring in the field. There were rustles and whistles she did not recognise. Comma spent the first night of her marriage sleepless.

Slip told her that it was quail season. His plan was to fashion nets to trap and hunt the birds at night. The hunting field was about an hour's bike ride from their home. Slip had discovered it on one of his exploratory rides, something she had never heard of before. Her younger brothers liked to roam the countryside, but they had never been allowed to go far, and the older boys she knew didn't have time for aimless wandering. Slip explained his plans for the day to her, but Comma did not feel she could question him further. Neither did he ask what she planned to do with her day.

Comma prepared breakfast and lunch, cleaned their house, and then walked over to help Slip's mother with her chores and the preparations for the dinner they were to all eat together at the Nguyễn house. Slip's mother was extraordinarily kind, given how often mothers-in-law enslaved their sons' brides. She was also more independent and capable than Comma's own mother; her house was already in order. She did not need Comma to do much. So when Slip brought up the quail-hunting, Comma offered to sell the birds at the land market, especially as they did not have an extra boat for her to go to the floating market.

After spending the day building nets and hooks, Slip collected baskets from his family's house and left to hunt after dinner. Comma watched him ride off until she could no longer make out his silhouette. She couldn't help thinking that Slip had chosen to go out at night to avoid her. He had not raised the subject of sex and still had not touched her. And now it was the second night of their marriage and he was not even in the house. To comfort herself, she brewed the floral tea before bed. Because she had barely slept the night before, she only had to listen to the strange cicadas for a moment before she fell asleep.

When Comma woke the next morning, Slip was beside her in the bed. She did not know when he had returned. Wild flapping sounds came from outside. When she went outside, she found about thirty quail in a bamboo pen that Slip must have built yesterday as well. She felt a flush of pride, which immediately turned to embarrassment, as she realised that he was perhaps not truly her husband yet.

She went to make their coffee and breakfast. The sounds of the cooking woke Slip, who appeared in their outside kitchen.

'That's an incredible lot of quail!' she said.

'Isn't it!' It was a kind smile, a real smile. Or was he just being polite, she wondered.

'They look so lively, they must have the run of the field out there,' she said, knowing that the more chicken and quail ran, the tastier their meat was.

'They'll be delicious. We'll save one to bring over to my

mother's for dinner,' said Slip. 'Are you sure you can sell these at the land market? Do you need help?'

'Yes, I'll be fine. I used to sell at the markets every day with my sister,' said Comma.

'That's right,' he said, with a hint of apology. 'If you need anything, I can help you.'

She could sense his polite manner taking over.

'I'll be fine. You should get some rest. Were you out there all night?' said Comma.

'Yes, I think I will rest. It was almost dawn when I returned,' said Slip.

So they went their separate ways. Comma was glad to have something to do. There were too many quail to bike over herself, so she borrowed a large wooden cart from the Nguyễn property. She secured the quail tightly in two baskets and wheeled the squawking, flapping lot over to the land market, which was much closer to the Nguyễns' than to her family's house. Now that she was a married woman, Comma arrived at the market with her hair in a bun instead of braids.

The quail were a success and sold out quickly. No one else at the market had quails as large and energetic as Comma's. Shoppers also stopped by her stall to congratulate her on the marriage. That night, as Comma and Slip's quails were cooked in thirty-odd homes in Cai Lậy, the tastiness of the meat assured the province that the marriage must be a very blessed one.

For the next four weeks, Comma and Slip busied themselves

with quail. He was gone every night after dinner, she went to sleep alone, he came back before dawn, and as he slept during the day, she went out and sold all the quail at the market. He had found a way to attach larger baskets to the back of his bike to transport more quail home. 'There are as many quail out there as I want,' he said. They were making a great profit, but the work was not enough to distract Comma from her worries.

She could not tell anyone that she and Slip had still not had sex. She could not speak about it with someone from his family, and she would not be able to visit her own family for at least another month. It was a bad sign for a bride to come back to her mother's house too early; it was seen as disrespectful to the groom's family. She wasn't sure, anyway, that she could really discuss this with Apostrophe, and Comma could not broach the subject with her mother, who would only be made uncomfortable.

Although Comma did not engage in gossip, she knew at least that it was uncommon for a new couple not to have sex. From what she gathered, grooms could not keep their hands off their new brides. What cruel coincidence was it that she, the introverted and cool-headed girl, had found herself married to a strangely dispassionate boy? He was, she was discovering, different from most people she knew. It was forgivable for a male not to be *lanh*, but most men in Cai Lậy were even louder than that, more impulsive. She did not want a brash husband, but she had not imagined a marriage like this. Until now, she had been proud of living without the wild

Mekong passion—it made her a good daughter and gave her a steady hand in running the household. Comma had always been ready for anything, and weathered everything. But could she really live without passion for the rest of her life?

And then the threats turned up again. Several times she found voodoo dolls in her pockets, needles stuck in the vagina. Other times she found notes with locks of hair, or in a pool of spit, or amongst fingernails. They were more frequent now. Was the sender desperate, she asked herself, or was it for fun? She found them all while Slip was away. And he was so often away. She passed on three of the notes to Apostrophe at the land market, and received translations back the next day.

I WILL SLASH UP YOUR VAGINA.

HE WILL LEAVE YOU, YOU UGLY HAG.

HE WILL NEVER LOVE YOU.

Comma was no longer frightened by these threats. The mystery woman had not done anything, despite her promise to kill Comma before the wedding. But the threats irritated her. They seemed to mock her. Did the woman know that she and Slip still had not consummated their marriage? The woman obviously hung about the house, after all—she placed the notes in the clothes Comma left to dry in the backyard. Did she know, as Comma knew, that Slip did not love Comma? Did the mystery woman know—it panicked Comma even to say it in her head—that Comma did not love Slip, and was not sure that she was even capable of it? The threats were proof of an intensity of feeling somewhere out there, the very thing that was lacking between the newlywed couple.

One night Comma stayed up until Slip came home, around dawn. She dared to watch as he undressed with his back to her, gazing at the broad shoulders admired by so many women in Cai Lậy, and at his muscles rippling in the faint light. She shifted in the bed as he approached, to let him know she was awake.

'Sorry, did I wake you?' he whispered.

'No, I was already awake.'

'Well, sorry. Go back to sleep,' he said, crawling under the blanket gingerly.

Comma turned on her side so that she could still see him. His eyes were closed. Resolutely, she thought. What was wrong? She wished she could ask him. Maybe it was up to her to reach out for him. But clearly he did not want her to. In the shut eyes and perfectly still form—when he really could not be asleep yet!—it was obvious he did not want anything to happen between them. But she was desperate for some kind of answer.

'I want to go with you next time,' said Comma.

His eyes fluttered open. 'What? Where?'

'Quail-hunting with you,' she said.

'You do?' he said slowly. Lying on his back, he looked up at the ceiling.

'I can be helpful,' said Comma. 'And I want to see what it's like.'

'It won't be easy for you,' he said.

'I don't mind. I can keep up,' said Comma.

'It takes most of the night,' he said.

'I know.'

He was silent for a while longer. 'If you're sure,' he said.

'I'm sure.'

Eventually his eyes closed again, and then fluttered open, as though he was bracing for more queries from her. Comma turned away, onto her back. Her heart was racing, and she hoped he couldn't tell. She wondered if the mystery woman or the greedy spirits of the Mekong were nearby that night, and whether they had heard Comma begin to fight for Slip.

Comma and Slip were to set out quail-hunting the next night. After she came home from the land market, with all quail sold out as expected, she imagined he might suggest she was tired from the work and should stay home. But he didn't, and she was glad. There were other ways he could stymie their plan— by mentioning it to his parents at dinner, for example. The Nguyễn parents would have objected to the idea and Comma would have been obliged to obey them. But he didn't bring it up. Perhaps he hoped she had forgotten?

After they had walked home from dinner, Comma went outside to bring the laundry in. She no longer left it out to dry at night, tired of having to check her pockets for voodoo dolls and needles. Folding clothes inside the house, she was again surprised by how strongly Slip's scent stayed in his shirts, so much stronger than how he smelt in person. She heard him fiddling in the kitchen, then the whistle of boiling water. He brought in two cups, the steel Vietnamese *phin* coffee filter on top of each cup.

'You better have some coffee, then,' he said.

'Thank you.'

He sat down next to her. They said nothing as the coffee dripped smoothly and she finished folding. He got up and put away the piles of clothes and the pegs.

'Ready?' he asked when he was done.

'Ready.'

Outside, as he fastened his basket to his bike, she started to do the same with hers.

'You don't need to bring another basket—mine is big enough,' said Slip.

'I don't mind.'

'It's a really long ride out there and tough to carry the quail home,' he said.

'We can take more this way,' she replied.

He stopped moving, about to object further, but instead he watched her finish knotting the rope. He had not seen her handiwork before, as he usually took his nap while she got her cart ready for the market. In truth, Comma was apprehensive about the night. She had never ridden that far or been to wild places, and never even stayed up all night. But the rope was something she knew how to do well and she didn't want to show any hesitation. When she had finished the knots, she looked at him and he nodded.

Slip mounted his bike and led them to the main path by the River Ba Rại. As she followed him, Comma decided that she liked riding at night. It felt faster than usual, and she was excited by the shadows of the trees and the large tropical leaves looming towards her as she sped along. Soon they were out of the town and travelling down open dirt roads. They rode on for miles.

The wind slapped at Comma. Every now and then her fingers grew stiff around the bike handles and she had to wriggle them back to life. Slip looked back at her frequently. The rapid twist of his head, and the flash of his face, made him look bewildered, as if he was trying to believe she was really there. Comma resolved to keep up with him, but her legs were not used to the exercise and her calves were cramping painfully.

They left the river and the wide road and turned down a narrow, raised dirt path into a rice paddy. After the rice paddy came wild grass, a pond, and then Slip stopped. The moment Comma dismounted, her legs cramped so much that she wanted to fall to her knees. But she disguised it from Slip, and only massaged her legs when he wasn't looking.

Slip reached into his basket and took out several rings of bamboo that he looped around his neck, like giant necklaces, along with a handful of small nets that he looped around his elbows. The strands of the nets were fine and white; Comma could barely see them in the darkness.

'Traps for the birds,' he explained.

She nodded awkwardly, feeling exposed out there in the middle of the night on strange land. The ride had been much further than she had expected. But the moon was out and Comma imagined that there was no other place in the world where a person could see so many stars.

She followed Slip as he walked among the tall grass. He squatted down, flexed the bamboo into an arc and inserted it into the dirt. Then he pried a net from the other tangled nets, and tugged it down both sides of the bamboo arc, as if he was putting a shirt on a toddler. After he had laid down four nets, Comma spoke up.

'Let me try—I think I know how it works,' she said.

He handed her half of the remaining bamboo and nets. He stood by to watch her lay her first trap. Once she was finished, he squatted next to her and shook the bamboo, testing its strength. He nodded approvingly.

'Good. Make sure the net reaches all the way down, so that it doesn't spring up,' he said.

Comma found the work soothing. After the first fifteen traps, Slip took longer bamboo strips out of the basket and they laid down the larger nets.

Then he walked her back to the raised dirt road, where they could observe the traps. He sat down and rested his wrists on his knees, looking satisfied. Comma sat beside him, flexing her legs out carefully and wincing.

'Now we wait,' he said.

Comma grew tenser with every passing minute. Her ears strained for the approach of the quails. But none came. Slip had brought home so many, there must be a squall of them, but where were they? Her head swam with the possibilities of what could happen between her and Slip. Why had she insisted on coming tonight, anyway? What was it that she planned to do out here that would be different from what had been happening at home? Even if there were quail, Comma could not bear the thought of merely catching quail and biking all the way back, only for each of them to climb into bed with the blanket flat between them. Not without an explanation— or *something*.

Several times, over the long hours, she almost spoke. Finally, when she was about to burst out with questions, Slip held up his hand.

'A quail is coming,' he whispered breathlessly.

He pointed to the left of the field: a patch of grass blades was moving and then a round, brown quail emerged. Comma screamed in excitement, her hand clutching Slip's sleeve as they watched the quail run straight into one of their traps: a little soccer ball in the darkness. As the quail struggled, making a ruckus, the net tangled until the bird was stuck.

Comma laughed from relief, and from the thrill of the catch. In this mood, she was ready again to say something to Slip, anything, but he was already clutching at her arm.

'Look! More!' he cried.

Close to where their first quail was trapped, three more approached, tumbling down the hill, wound up in their own traps.

'The noise of one quail attracts the others,' Slip explained.

He cupped his fingers around his mouth and let out a high-pitched clucking, imitating the quails. He looked at Comma, inviting her to join in. Comma laughed, disarmed. She cupped her fingers to her mouth and tried her own clucking, a more warbled version, which she thought sounded closer to the call of the awkward, inelegant quail. Slip was smiling at her. In the dark, far from their hometown, he looked genuinely happy for the first time. And then he looked shy. She had been waiting for this, to be let into his private world.

They kissed, slowly and shyly, as the quails arrived in swarms. The birds' chorus of riotous clucking in front of the couple disturbed the cicadas, which were still singing out of rhythm.

Hours later, once the quail were inside the baskets, Comma taught Slip how to tie the baskets to their bikes her way, which they agreed was more secure. Later still, down the wide dirt road, Comma called out and asked if they could stop. She confessed that her legs were cramping and that the ride was much more difficult with a load of squirming quail. They had caught many more quail than they needed, so Slip carefully untangled them, bird by bird, and released half the quail from Comma's basket. Comma and Slip watched ten or so birds waddle away at full speed.

Comma rode in front the rest of the way home, so that she could set the speed. She wasn't sure of the direction, but guessed which fork in the road to take and found that she remembered the trees and houses they had passed earlier. Each time she turned to look back at Slip, a small, familiar face in the middle of the shadowy Mekong wilderness, he seemed a little more real to her. Sometimes he was looking out at the fields and streams beside them; sometimes he was already smiling back at her.

Comma did not know yet that each time she turned around to look at Slip in the days and years to come, it would be different. Even later that day, it would be different, when they arrived home, and, in the uncertain, hushed hour before dawn, they reached for each other. It would be different a year later, after they had put their firstborn son down to sleep, and whispered his secret, beautiful name to each other in their shared private world. She did not know yet that each of these moments of theirs, decades of them, would grow and cascade until, finally, Slip would pass away, Comma following only months later, tethered by her wild, mad, Mekong love.

Dinosaurs

The bathroom had pink tiles. That was one thing. Another thing I remember is the small, oblong window above the sink. Too small to let a body through, but enough of a gap to let the Buenos Aires songs float in, and keep floating in. It was a Tuesday night. I remember because, as I was pissing into the urinal, a guy walked past outside, singing, 'Saturday, Saturday, Saturday, oh Saturday night is over.' I heard him as if he was right next to me. The open window was just above my head, no flyscreen or glass. I remember because I was drunk and I thought, *That at least is true: it is Tuesday, and so Saturday night is over*. It was true like so very few things are.

That's what I was thinking, so I would have noticed if Gabo had come in. Or if Gabo had been there, because I would have wanted to talk to someone about how it was Tuesday, and Saturday night was over. I'm just trying to explain what goes through my head when I've been drinking like that: that's the way I think then, definitely, even if not properly. Definitely, Gabo did not come through the bathroom.

It was five months ago, the night Juan did a set on his own, or rather, with a different band. He was all right. He was doing acoustic, all soft and mellow, pop song choruses, and a guitar around his neck. Juan figured he was a handsome guy and, back then, all the romantic guys were singing bossa nova like the Brazilians.

Juan brought a new girl to the bar that night, this skinny brunette. I don't remember her name. She was leaning forward on her chair listening to Juan, not talking to any of us guys, even though she was sitting at our table. She was like a bird, with a dainty chin and wet eyes, a real sad face, although she laughed a lot, kind of nervously. She looked miserable, but maybe that's just the way her face was.

The other night, when everyone was talking about Gabo, she asked me straight up:

'You were with him that night, weren't you, Manu?'

It was the first time she'd spoken to me directly.

'We were all with him. He was with us.'

'But you were.' She stopped. 'You were *with* him, weren't you?'

Then I wanted to kill her, and it must have showed because

she took off. I had been on a short fuse. Everyone wanted to ask me about Gabo, but for some reason she made me really angry. Maybe she was embarrassed that she couldn't say outright that we were fucking, Gabo and I. But that's all it was between us, and it wasn't a big deal. Or maybe it was just her sad bird-eyes that set me off.

We all met Gabo at the University of Buenos Aires in July last year. The student union Juventud Guevarista held a midnight rally, the first of many. Mostly speeches and poems, young kids in jeans, manifestos sticking out of their back pockets. They asked us to do some songs. Rafael's sister was in the Guevaristas and that's how they knew our band.

I can't remember the set list, because I had already got high while the kids were giving their speeches and reading from Che or something. So we got up and started playing, and in the middle of a song I forgot what came next. I was playing bass as well as singing, and I got stuck on two notes for about five minutes. I think it was D flat and E and I just played D flat-E, D flat-E, D flat-E over and over. The guys were freaking out.

But then I started singing, 'Something, there's something, something's in the water,' and I played that infernal bass line again. It sounded like it was all an accident, but I sang it because I'd been thinking about this stuff for a while. I sang, 'There's something in the water, you know, something in the water.' The kids loved it.

We were doing what we'd heard was going on in the Tucumán music scene. Los Perros had a song about building a raft and escaping, and Almendra was doing a song about ice falling over the city, freezing the city when everybody is asleep. That was probably the best one I knew. The guys and I hadn't talked about this new music, but we played it and it was what the kids wanted, even though they hadn't asked for it. It was a time when nobody was saying anything much about anything, not really.

That was also before we really knew for sure that the military abductions were real. We'd heard rumours about some activists and students in Rosario disappearing. But nobody knew their names and it was all very uncertain. Maybe they were just hippies and left for the Andes one morning, or got broke and went back to their mothers in Tigre. You didn't know who you could ask, either.

But at this point the vultures hadn't come after musicians yet, or city kids. It was early enough that everyone was perversely excited about being involved in the protests. The whole thing was thrilling. Something was in the water.

After the Guevarista rally, we went drinking with some of the kids in La Boca. They were poets, carriers of the manifestos, and we had long conversations about things we didn't know much about. Gabo was one of the poets. I remember the first thing he said that night, because it made me wonder if he was retarded. We were all talking about Che, good Che, father of the young Latin American poets, saint of the Latin American bar room, and the baptism into his patronage by spirits, by which I mean Fernet spirits. We were loud and drunk. Suddenly Gabo said:

'I don't care if I fall.'

He hadn't spoken all night. His voice was high, stringy. It had to be—squeezed out of such a skinny body. But it was melodic, like he was reading poetry. Everybody stopped to wonder what the fuck.

'As long as somebody picks up my gun and starts shooting,' he said.

Then another student, recognising the Che quote, shouted, and squeezed Gabo's shoulders, rumpling his dark green sweater so that a section of his collarbone was revealed. I looked at him, and felt uncharacteristically shy when he stared back at me. He was a pale guy, ginger hair, slender with almond eyes like an Asian. He was the most delicate person I've ever seen, and the most serious.

In bed, he embarrassed me with his seriousness. We left the bar, and I took him with me: his serious looks were seductive, and I wanted to reward him for his Che quote and for the respect the other students clearly had for him. But I was unsure, because he gave me no signals. Even when he started taking his clothes off, slowly, studiously, it was as if I wasn't there, as if his sole focus was on folding his sweater, his khaki pants, his thin T-shirt and his cotton underpants. I was embarrassed again by his skinny body. I stood watching him. I didn't feel as if I could touch him. I felt strange. That was Gabo's trick: he made me feel strange and melancholy. But mostly I was just wondering what the fuck, is he retarded or a poet? Then I got angry at myself for feeling strange and went after him.

Gabo wrote a song for us in September, or was it November? He'd been at a lot of our gigs. He'd come from the university and sit with the other kids, not drinking or talking, but they always saved a seat for him and fell silent when he spoke, like he was their secret god. I still don't really get it. We were hanging out with the university kids a lot by then, and some other odd people who talked about rock and poetry—and who drank a lot, of course—just hanging out, like we were all waiting for something to happen.

After 'Something in the Water', the guys and I only played songs like that. New songs, nothing sentimental anymore. Only about the things that nobody was talking about. Pablo knew another student poet, Maria; he was sleeping with her. She wrote an insane song for us called 'Mister Scissors', about a guy who cut out scenes from a film that starred his lover, editing and rearranging the clips. Then one night he comes home and cuts her up in bed. It was good, really freaky. The first night we rehearsed it, Maria was standing next to the stage, right in front of me, and she kept shrieking, 'Louder! Louder! Louder!' I paid attention to her, because honestly I was scared of her, and because the song has a climax in which everything is shrieking, like the lover in the song when she's being cut up. I didn't know how Pablo could get into bed with someone like Maria, but it was good, because we started getting more attention with that song.

Maybe Gabo wrote a song for us because he was jealous of Maria's success.

'I wrote you a song,' he said suddenly, in the middle of the night, as if an alarm had gone off. He got up and walked over to the window ledge, where he picked up a piece of folded paper, then came back to bed and handed it to me.

He didn't have handwriting like a poet; his letters were big and childlike. The song was about dinosaurs.

'Read it slowly,' he said, his naked body beside me. That wasn't hard because my hangover was on the way.

'*Imagine the dinosaurs in your streets, imagine the dinosaurs in your bed, imagine the dinosaurs disappear.*'

'Slowly, slowly.'

'*The dinosaurs will disappear, the dinosaurs will disappear,*' I read.

I didn't sing it; I was too tired. But Gabo nodded, his expression serious. In my stupor, the song made sense, although in the morning it sounded a bit odd. But by then I trusted him enough, this strange, skinny god of the young poets, and the song became our greatest hit.

We performed 'Dinosaurs' in Tucumán in November. It was a huge gig. They called it a happening, and all the kids came down for it from Buenos Aires and Rosario, even Santa Fe and Montevideo. The best bands were there; it was a big deal. Almendra were there. They knew about our dinosaur song, just like we knew about their snow song. They even looked like us, four haggard guys in their twenties like they didn't have a mattress between them, or a mother. We had Juan, though. Nobody had a guy as handsome as Juan.

Gabo travelled with us, nothing special. I mean, not with me. A group of Buenos Aires students had started coming everywhere with us, including Gabo and Maria, who was sleeping with Juan by then. A couple days before we left for Tucumán, I passed a kiosko in Buenos Aires that sold kids' books alongside the chips and candy. Books like *The Little Prince* and *Mafalda*, and a book about dinosaurs. When I saw it, I had to buy it. But it felt like a stupid idea once I'd brought it home, so I gave it to Gabo.

He took the book gently, as if it would fall apart. Impatient, I grabbed it back and flipped over to the page I'd flagged.

'This one is you,' I said, pointing. '*Apatosaurus*.'

It was one of the vegetarian dinosaurs, with scaly skin and a long skinny neck that made me think of Gabo's body.

He stared at the page, then said, 'You are not one at all.'

I was angry for a second, and then I realised it didn't matter. It was just a stupid kids' book. But if I was one, I think I would be a big flying Quetzalcoatlus.

Things got really crazy after the Tucumán performance. There were thousands of people in the hall, and even more outside on the grass. Everyone was camping because the hostels were full. Nobody slept that weekend anyway, except with each other. I didn't see Gabo again because the band was constantly swarmed by fans, and also I was blind drunk the whole time. We had made it then, really made it. We played 'Dinosaurs' over and over, every day, and it was great every time, every-body wanted to hear it, over and over. The kids worshipped us and chanted our names. New kids came back to Buenos Aires with us, along with some of the same faces, but it was hard to keep track because, like I said, I was drunk the whole time and there were a lot of people around.

The last time anyone saw Gabo was on the Tuesday. We were out drinking at some bar in Palermo, the guys, Maria and the kids who came along with us. Gabo didn't come home that night or the next, or the next, and soon we realised that we had seen him for the last time. No one could talk about anything else; we were really scared. The guys in the band asked me about it. Did I know where he lived? Did he seem scared around that time? Did it seem as if he knew what was going to happen?

Once, the guys and I all sat down and talked about what we remembered of that night.

'He left early.'

'He was strange that night.'

'He's always strange.'

'The bathroom had pink tiles,' I told them.

I was passed out in the bathroom when Gabo left, on his own. I must have been there a long time, because everyone thought I had left too. But I was sitting in the bathroom, staring at the pink tiles, dizzy.

In the end, we didn't figure out anything and didn't feel any better. We didn't meet to play anymore. There always seemed to be something more important to do, although I didn't really have anything to do, except drink.

By the end of the month, Juan and Maria left to go to Juan's country home. They didn't tell us where it was exactly, and we didn't talk about the band again. Nobody talked much. There was a lot of moving around, and I saw Pablo and Rafael a couple more times. But two or three months after that Tuesday night, I knocked on Pablo's door and got no answer. The neighbours told me that no one lived there anymore. So then I was alone most of the time.

One night, I found myself in the same bar again. I didn't mean to go there; I didn't want to see that place ever again. At first, I didn't recognise the place. It was like any dingy dive in Palermo, a neon burger sign out front—the same neon burger sign that hung outside a couple of spots I know in the city.

I sat at a low table, unreasonably low for an average adult. I felt overgrown and sad. The seats were so close to the floor that my knees hung out to the sides. I forgot to order a burger and drank a lot of beer instead.

After a while, I began to feel bloated and my knees were cramping, as if the table was sinking. Yes, I must have been drunk. The vertigo gave me the sensation that I was heading for the floor, not like an upright person falling over, but as if I was swelling and swallowing up the furniture.

I made myself get up and go to the bathroom. When I washed my hands, I looked up and saw the small, oblong window and started screaming. The vertigo, or whatever it was, meant that I filled up the room. I had a bird's eye view of the tiny bathroom: it had white tiles, although I knew it was the same bathroom as that night. I checked and, even though I was swollen and huge, it was obvious that a person could have fitted through the window. Then I heard bird songs and a woman's voice.

'You were with him that night, weren't you, Manu?'

It was Maria's voice, Maria with the sad bird-eyes, but why didn't I know it? And I understood then why the tiles were pink that night and why I spent such a long time staring at them and never forgot that they were pink. The room swelled with bird songs, with Maria's voice, and I thought I might die, but then it passed. I pissed. I was sitting back on the toilet seat. I kept pissing and the room deflated, so did I, and the bird songs faded. I smelled fried meat and remembered that I had ordered a burger after all, and that I was ravenous, so I washed my hands again and went back to the bar, which looked the same, and it was like nothing had happened. Nothing could have happened at all, not really.

I Just Want to Hear You Say It

It is no joy to write about what has already happened. But the story of this girl must persist because it already has. At some point, when we are in the thick of it, you may be tempted to believe that I have a choice, but you should not; I do not. Her name is damned and I cannot forget her. The dumb girl muttering songs by the highway has to live, though she did not ask for it. She only lives because she wakes up in the morning. That is understood, there is no other way.

Linh Ngô knew two things about herself. One, she liked Goody elastics. Two, she was a waitress. Today the café was empty and Linh lay rocking in a hammock, one brown leg sticking out, as she played with a Goody elastic. She always had one around her wrist and flicked it idly against her skin, smacking her lips like a fish, imitating the sound.

'What kind of hair elastics do you use?' she imagined somebody asking. 'Goody,' she would reply. She kicked out and the hammock rocked again. Linh turned dumb conversations in her head, round and about, all day. In my weaker moments, I have wanted something more for her. Sometimes, for an enchanting moment in her sleep, she might have had dreams. I've seen her finger her bottom lip softly, more tenderly than in her waking world, before snapping awake. I found it almost grotesque, like fat people fucking, or spit in your soup.

Linh had always been a Ngày Mới girl. An hour down the freeway from Sài Gòn, Ngày Mới province started around an open market square that smouldered at night with fried flour cakes and smoked shrimp. Cement roads wound uncertainly from the square and halted suddenly at dirt roads. There the farmlands began, rough patches of potatoes in between squares of sap trees. And then the long, dense sugarcane fields. Save for posters of Hồ Chí Minh around the market square, Ngày Mới was curiously unchanged by the war. Some of its people had died on the battlefield, some in the tunnels in their backyards, but the rest eked out lives as desperate and thirsty as anyone could remember.

Linh had been waitressing for three years, since she was fourteen. She had to give up her mother's sewing work; it left her dazed. The thread's end, rolling out and aiming for a needle's eye, infuriated her to tears. She often lost track of the chalk line down a sheet of cotton and ran the needle askew, sawing madly in and out of the cloth. The café work came more easily to Linh. Soaping plates and wiping stains seemed as natural as the need to eat.

Her mother was really so different. Nga had been running needles down sheets of cotton all her life. She leaned closer to the cloth as the years added on, her eyes straining. Through the course of the day, she moved around the room to follow a streak of light from the window. Her arms grew hard as she rearranged the work table every two hours, the wooden bed twice a day, and stacks of clothes in and out the door every day.

Their prayer house and the family graveyard were at the end of the irrigation stream. On New Year's Eve, Linh and Nga went to clean the prayer house before joining everybody at temple. Linh was wearing Nga's blouse, the button-down one that Nga saved for special occasions. It was a present from Sài Gòn before 1975 and Nga still kept it in the clear plastic wrapping.

'What kind of girl forgets to iron her clothes?' Nga hissed, tugging the ends of the blouse so that Linh stumbled forward. Nga's bony hands pressed against her daughter's hips. If Nga lifted the cloth, she would have seen red marks in the shape of fingers.

'You're hurting me,' Linh said as she twisted out of Nga's hands.

Nga raised her right arm, baring a line of muscle that ran down to the inside of her elbow, and slapped Linh hard on the face.

'Remember your manners. Don't make me look like I've raised a bad child,' Nga said.

Linh kept silent as Nga pulled her hair into a tight ponytail and made her urinate before they left. At the prayer house, they swept the floor and tied marigolds to the ancestors' portraits. Although the prayer house was made of cement, not marble or stone, this edifice for the dead was the only remnant of modest wealth in the family. It strikes me as a more pathetic scene than to have found Linh and her mother by the kind of dug-up dirt graves they would eventually be buried in. It helps me to pinpoint that quality in my girl: if there was a good memory for her, it has already been used up by somebody else.

Linh rocked as she prayed, touching her forehead to the ground. Ditties filled her head, and she sang to the rhythm of her rocking. *Raised-a-bad-child, raised-a-bad-child, raised-a-bad-child. Going-to-temple, going-to-temple, going-to-temple.* She looked at Nga, who was praying in a stream of hisses, her dutiful back snapping up and down. A pigeon crept to Nga's side, towards the bag of moon cakes. Linh twisted her head to the side. Her neck cricked and the pigeon fled. Soon the song was *a-pretty-bird-bird, a pretty-bird-bird, a-birdy-bird-bird-bird-bird.*

Linh made a friend that year. The staff at Hòa Trân Café was mostly a mix of the owner's distant relatives, many of them much older than Linh. But the new girl was only twenty. Trang had full breasts and dressed like a Sài Gòn girl: blue jeans and tight T-shirts studded with plastic beads. She kept a mobile phone in her back pocket—when she walked, it gave you the urge to grab her arse to stop the phone from falling out.

'I curl my hair with wet cloth,' said Trang. She liked to give advice.

They were sorting through fruit pulp in the kitchen to reuse for juice. Linh rubbed some papaya between her fingers and the juice ran down to her elbow. Like the ants she sometimes found suffocated in sugarcane mulch, she knew that sweetness was for touching, but she also knew that it was not for her.

'Like this,' said Trang. She wiped her hands on her jeans and reached up to twist a lock of her hair. 'You fold the hair over and over, tie it with some cloth, and it's all done when you wake up.'

Trang bounced the curl. A smear of juice glistened in her hair. It shone against the sweat on her skin, which was dark and bubbling with pimples.

'It's really easy when you have thick hair like me. But your hair is thin and limp, I don't know if it would suit you,' said Trang.

It did not occur to Linh to respond. She was satisfied with watching Trang. She liked the soft part of Trang's belly, the slight curve out to the hips that was more evident when she wore fitted shirts. She liked the bright colours Trang wore: in the plastic beads on her shirt, in her lipstick, and in the alligator clips in her hair. Sometimes she wore coloured eyeshadow. When Trang moved, she was a whirl of colour and shine.

'That's why Vinh makes you tie your hair up,' said Trang.

Vinh was the head chef.

'It's the type of hair that people find in their soup. It makes them sick.'

It still didn't occur to Linh to say anything.

But something happened after months of studying Trang. One evening, as Linh was walking home along the freeway, she looked sideways to the Vương' photocopy shop, one of the few shopfronts made of glass, and saw her reflection. She saw the dark-streaked face and the thick, ruddy lips. The hard clusters of pimples had grown so thick that her cheeks seemed like two raised lumpy disks. Her eyes were growing further apart as she got older. She was startled by the ugliness of her image and didn't know what to do. Up until this moment, she thought of her appearance as a composition of the same elements other girls had: middle-parted hair (Nga said modest girls didn't wear side-parts), a face that needed to be washed in the morning, forearms grown wide from carrying plates. Now Linh realised that other people would not like to look at her. And there was nothing she could do to fix this.

In the murkiness of the glass, the shadow of her self-hatred lurked behind Linh's silhouette and she shuddered to shake it off.

I felt as if I could hear the voice inside her head and I dared her to say something. What does a girl say when she first learns to be disgusted by herself? I fantasised an anger that would lash my cheek, that would claw so tightly it would pierce my skin. But her distress coughed and sputtered. It was a long shot anyway. What kind of pain is more common, and more dull, than self-hatred? Linh looked away and hurried home.

Then it was spring and the time for peanuts. Linh had already gone to peanut-pulling nights twice that month. The Lý family were hasty and shelled too early, but the Nguyễns' peanuts were perfect, large and sweet. On those warm, blue nights, the farmyards were full of squatting women gossiping as they shook peanuts out of the bushes. Sometimes, with a large crop like the Hồs had two springs ago, the women would stay all through the night. Everyone took a share when the harvest was finished.

It was work that suited Linh. The night came and cooled the sweat of the day. At first, the stalks pricked, then routine set in, peanuts snapping and sliding off under her fingers like the *tut-tuts* of the women, who approved of so few other women. *Tut-tut*, bad blood, *tut-tut*, that devil child, *tut-tut*, the parents' fault, *tut-tut*, that brazen slut. Linh was of little interest to them. What a shame about her face, they said, but she can work, yes? She's a good girl. She stays home and she works. Linh never spoke and was happy to work for hours.

She liked the walks back home too, in the new hours of the day. The tall grasses talked to each other, rustling, unseen. The mud was cold and the buffaloes rolled gently in their sleep. Pots scraped as mothers opened their houses, trying not to wake the children. For a moment, the air in Ngày Mới, always sweet and dense with the scent of sugarcane, was cut through with the dawn's chill. But for the ditties she sang in her head, Linh's mind was empty as she walked.

That night everyone was going to Cậu Tắm's farm for shelling. Nga had woken at sunrise to start sewing so that she could finish by evening.

'Cậu Tắm's boys have already started taking the roots out. A really good batch, they say,' said Nga.

She had packed their food for the night, two balls of sticky rice and a packet of boiled peanuts with sesame sugar.

'We start at eight, and we should be finished before dawn,' continued Nga.

There was no answer from Linh, who sat still on the edge of the bed. Nga came over and smacked Linh's head with her palm.

'Are you dumb? Get moving!' Nga shouted.

'I'm sick,' said Linh. Her Ngày Mới accent sounded like like oil boiling. Not the musical bubbling of schoolgirls and marketeers, but bursts from the roiling pot. She was often surprised by her own voice. That is why somebody must speak for her, but it is not easy. It is like prying open an oyster with my nails and eating the live bits inside.

Nga felt her daughter's forehead.

'No, my stomach is sick. I have my period,' said Linh.

'The devil,' cursed Nga. 'What kind of daughter is so lazy.'

Nga narrowed her eyes and scrutinised Linh's crotch. Nga's periods were always light, sometimes no more than a few specks of blood.

'Fine, stay home,' Nga said finally. 'But it will bring shame

114

on me. What kind of a daughter will everyone think I have raised?'

She opened the plastic bag and gave Linh a ball of sticky rice and the sesame packet.

'And don't sit there like a dumb lump—you can rub the pots and clean out the altar,' said Nga.

She turned around one last time to smooth the baby hairs off Linh's forehead, then left the house.

Linh stayed frozen on the edge of the bed. The words of a dutiful response bubbled somewhere at the base of her throat, then petered out. She crept across the room and fiddled with the scraps of Nga's sewing. She picked out a few extra strips of fabric and went into the backyard to wet them under the tap, looking about as she squatted and held the limp cotton under the water. Back at the edge of the bed, she sat cross-legged and fumbled with her hair, trying to tie the cloth and make curls the way Trang had shown her. But her fingers were stiff and clumsy and her hair tangled.

She threw the wet strips aside, pulled her legs up close and hugged the soles of her feet. She sat like this for a long time, and forgot about the pots and the altar. The ball of sticky rice had rolled and settled in the middle of the sunken mattress. There was nothing in her head, but out of habit she gurgled to a listless rhythm, her expression slack. She was pathetic, mumbling and rocking, her hands clutching her feet. I should have given her a moment alone. But I was curious: what fancies might she have for the night? It was always these tremors of inclination that I found most pitiful.

When she started moving again, Linh surprised herself by taking her jacket and heading out the door. She had never lied to Nga before.

Hòa Trân Café was perched on the edge of the cement freeway, at the border of Ngày Mới. A yellow banner stretched across the entrance of the café, letters spelt out in red serif type. Serifs that were faded but classic, rippling in the wind. Underneath was the forever slogan: 'Karaoke special this Thursday night only!' The Sài Gòn girls dismounted from their scooters beneath the banner, slid off their driving gloves and looked around the yard for a table with a view. Near the back was a small pond filled with yellow fish.

Linh had never seen the café at night, bathed like this in blueish light. The yard smelled of dried squid and beer. She felt intimidated. She watched a man sitting in her favourite hammock, one red hand gripping his thigh as he talked to his friends. His other hand clutched a can of beer. His fingers dug into the aluminium, crinkling it, but he seemed oblivious of the tension.

'Linh?'

She blinked when she saw Trang, whose colours were wilder in the blue light. Trang looked confused.

'What are you doing here?'

'You told me to come,' said Linh.

'No I didn't,' said Trang. 'I'm not even working tonight.'

Trang was not unkind. She just did not know what to do with Linh, who was still wearing her brown *bà ba*, the slacks and shirt ensemble that women wore for household chores. Linh was so *quê*, Trang thought. So country.

'Well, I guess you should sit down with us,' said Trang. They walked to the table where the man and his friends were sitting. Trang shrugged. 'She just showed up.'

Linh brought over a stool and sat as the men resumed their conversation. They were discussing the new female employees at work, the bottle-top factory in the industrial district. Linh didn't think about speaking, but she repeated their words in her head, *lips-like-a-whore, lips-like-a-whore, lips-like, lips-like, lips—*

'What's wrong with your friend?'

Linh shuddered as a hand grasped her side. It was Quân, the man sitting in her favourite hammock. He squeezed her ribs.

'Are you shy?' said Quân. He massaged a rib with his thumb and leaned in to give her his mug. 'It's okay, girl. Here, have my drink.'

He said girl, *con gái*, the same word for daughter. She drank from Quân's mug. She could think of nothing but his hand. Through his hand she felt the force of an opening to another world, where hands were used for something else. She did not know what it was, but it was not for sewing, cooking, cleaning or shelling peanuts. His thumb continued to grind up and down her rib as he talked to the others. She wondered if he had forgotten that he was holding on to her, as she sat, immobile. The pool of liquid in her stomach grew warmer and warmer, and the hand on her waist burned. Suddenly he turned to her and pushed his face up close. His breath was hot.

'Are you okay? Let's go for a walk, huh? Let's go for a walk, girl.'

In the depths of a grass field, he grabbed her by the shoulders, smiling.

'You like me, don't you? I saw you looking at me,' he said.

He dropped his gaze. Both his thumbs were now grinding her ribs in circles. Linh tried to concentrate, but she felt disconnected from her body. Her head was heavy. He spread his fingers out like a fan on her breasts.

Linh lurched to the side.

'What's wrong, girl?' he snarled. He dug his fingers into her breasts. 'What's wrong, huh?'

Linh looked down, bewildered to see the flesh of her breasts bulging in between his fingers.

'What are you doing?' she said.

'What am I *doing*?' he shouted. He held her by the throat with one hand and grabbed her crotch with the other. He pushed the cotton of her pants into her vulva.

'I want to go home,' she said.

'Shut up.'

'I want to go home.'

'Shut up!' he yelled, forcing her down and pushing her face into the dirt. 'And don't look at me.'

The pain was so bad it felt as if her head was splitting. He was at her side, jerking his groin against her thigh. She lay limp. He jerked over and over.

It is too cruel to watch and we shall turn away. At this point,

I am sick of myself. I have pried open the oyster with my nails; it was difficult and tedious. I have sweated through all my good clothes and the room is dense with the smell of stale toast. But I have always known that I could not resist my dumb, spit-in-the-soup girl. *Linh*. The vowel, rounded like monks humming, flicks off the tongue with a gentle *l* and reaches the forehead where it vibrates, *nh*. I am very sorry for what happened (and yet I am glad of her existence, so that it would not be me). Forgive me my weaknesses. In another life I will be born with boils for fingers and cataracts in my eyes.

But I must turn back. Here we are still with Linh, far in the south of ravaged Vietnam, in a nameless grass field that this man has chosen for our complicity.

She stayed limp as he took off his clothes, and then hers. They were both smeared with dirt. He picked at the lips of her vagina, the calluses on his thumb so hard she felt as if he would tear her. She lay horrified and curious. He climbed on top of her and pushed his penis inside. She whimpered, drooling into the dirt, and waited for him to stop. His belly smacked frantically against her thighs at first and then he seemed to tire, readjusting his grip from her breasts to her shoulders. He grunted and his thrusts became rougher. When he finally stopped, she watched as he pulled himself up to her face. His expression was loose and savage with exhaustion. He raised his teeth to her mouth and bit down on her bottom lip, where she kept her secret dream. Her lip tore and he collapsed beside her. Soon he was snoring. She kept still, terrified of waking him.

Linh woke up smelling sugar. The air was thick. She stared at the blades of sugarcane engulfing her, as though they had multiplied while she slept. She leaned over Quân's face, its evil exposed in sleep, and picked up the cigarette lighter lying by his head, fiddling with it as she waited for her vision to focus: in her mind's eye, the entire field caught fire and melted down to caramel.

She waded through sugary air all the way home. She had the peculiar feeling that, in this hour, the world was carved out for her singular misery. It was not yet dawn and all was quiet. There was no breeze to move the grass, kitchen windows were not yet open, and the roosters had been slain sometime in the night to stop the commencement of a new day. Even the ghosts of women and children who died howling for water in the tunnels beneath her could not be heard. Linh reached her house and pushed open the door.

Nga was sitting on the bed. She took one look at Linh and it was clear she knew everything. Nga's face was blotchy and her eyes bloodshot from crying. She let out a yelp, then started wailing at the walls. Her lips trembled uncontrollably. She clasped her thin elbows and cried and cried. Linh stood transfixed at the door. Nga cried maniacally, gasping for air, her throat rasping as she scraped at the skin on her arms.

Linh fell to her knees. From the ground, she caught sight of her face reflected in the pots lining the wall. Her revulsion shocked her out of her body.

'Of all the lives to be, why must I be me?'

Linh was instantly saved by the futility of her words, and was able to creep back inside her bones, to her cloistered misery.

This is where I depart. It has been exhausting and I am thoroughly disgusted with everyone involved, including myself. I will leave the girl alone. I think about what could have happened, if only I had left her as I first saw her. A silhouette of a skinny girl waiting by the highway. A name, and a hair elastic.

Abu Dhabi Gently

It was by chance that I had come to work in the United Arab Emirates instead of Oman. For that I was thankful. I had heard about Tanzanians who worked in Oman. My wife, Grace, read a story in the newspaper about a Tanzanian woman who went to work as a maid in Oman and was beaten by her mistress with wooden clothes hangers and raped by the husband when she tried to run away. I told Grace that it was not appropriate for her to read such stories. I was also irritated; she knew I had signed up to work overseas, so why was she trying to scare me? I asked my older cousins and they said there were lots of stories like this online, about Tanzanian maids in

Oman. Zanzibaris know how Omanis think of our people; we remember how they enslaved us in our own land, but the mainland Tanzanians forget easily. Still, my cousins said it was different for men. A man can take care of himself.

I am the only son of five children. I have four sisters: Neema, who is older, and Sophy, Mary and Faith, who are younger. I was the only one my parents sent to a private primary school, where they teach in English instead of Swahili, so that I could get into secondary school. Neema was also selected for secondary school, but she dropped out after Form 2. Neema was always smarter than me, and by the time I graduated, she had helped my parents open a beef shop in the Stone Town market. She and my father began to take the *dala dala*, the share van, to work at six in the morning. Neema took over all the negotiations with our suppliers. She was also good with customers, and with the finances.

The shop started to do well, much better than my parents' shop in the Mwanakwerekwe market, which my mother was now running on her own. It was because of Neema, and our new shop, that I finally got to marry Grace. Her family also lived in Mwanakwerekwe, but they were wealthier than us. Her father was a beef supplier from whom my parents bought produce, and they lived in a new house and had a car. Grace's father said that I had his permission to marry his daughter, but that a man who had completed his education should do more than sell food in a market.

For a year, I tried to look for a better job, while still keeping my part-time work at the slaughterhouse. I joined my friend

Saidy and his brothers in their garbage-collection business, but after the high season there wasn't enough work for all four of us and I had to leave. I briefly trained as a mechanic, but did not like the work. I considered getting a taxi licence. My English would be useful with the tourists, I knew Zanzibari roads well, and it would be comfortable work if I had air conditioning. But Grace's father, from whom we would have to borrow money, was not in favour. Finally, it was his idea for me to go overseas. His friend's son was doing construction work in Qatar and had now sent enough money home to build new houses for both his parents and his new wife.

Only once did Neema ask me if Grace was worth it.

'It is not just this one time,' she said, her voice strained. She was holding four pegs in her mouth as she hung out the washing. 'This man will always interfere with your life. He tries to control you. Are you sure this is what you want?'

I rubbed the callouses on my feet. Sitting cross-legged on a mat below the clothesline, looking up at Neema as she shook out clothes and sheets so smoothly, I felt like the chubby, fourteen-year-old boy who had come to her like this so many years ago, to tell her that I was being bullied at my new private school. She glanced down and it was as if she could see the thought passing through my mind.

'You have nothing to prove, Fredy.'

'I know.'

'No one calls you that name anymore.'

But she was wrong. Some of my friends still called me Fredy Mpole, not maliciously, simply because the name had stuck. I had been infatuated with the English teacher at my new school, Miss Irene, who had come from Dar es Salaam. For our diary-writing assignments, I wrote long, personal letters to her, sometimes four or five sickeningly detailed and emotional pages instead of the mandatory single page. When my classmates found them in the stack of homework on Miss Irene's desk, they passed them around, reading aloud sentences like 'On Friday you wore a long-sleeved black shirt' and 'I like your yellow earrings with bells on them'. I ran from the classroom. After Miss Irene had cajoled me to come back, she asked the class to be kinder to me, 'because Fredy is *mpole*'—'gentle'. Which only made things worse.

'*Je, Uole Ni Udahifu? Fua kwa wororo, usisugue wala kukamua,*' Neema said to me now, just like she did when I was younger. *But is it weak to be gentle? Be gentle, and do not knead or wring the fabric.* It used to be comforting, but as I grew older, any reminder of the name irritated me.

'I'm not a child anymore,' I snapped.

Neema looked down and nudged me playfully with her right foot.

'I know, Fredy. Lighten up.'

My father used to flinch in annoyance when he heard people calling me Fredy Mpole. And sometimes he yelled at me when I followed Neema around the house as she did chores, or when I was reading in my room—I was the only one with a room to myself. It didn't help that my teachers told him I was too quiet in class, and needed to make more friends. Maybe he was afraid I was gay. In any case, he thought I was spending too much time alone and needed to get out and work with my hands. So he got me the after-school shift in the slaughterhouse by the market. But the other workers were all older than me and didn't want to talk much. At school, I often still carried the metallic smell of blood from the slaughter-house, which just fuelled my classmates' teasing.

My father was so excited when, at nineteen, I introduced Grace to the family. She was my first girlfriend. She was sixteen, sweet and shy. She made me feel strong and protective, even though I was short, quiet and known as Fredy Mpole. Grace seemed to love me unquestionably; I didn't really believe then that anyone could love me like that. I agreed to sign up at the recruitment office to work overseas. Finally, Grace and I were allowed to get married.

A few months later, when they first called about the work in Oman, my legs and back were aching so badly that it was difficult to walk. And then I got a fever. I spent eleven days in bed, cold and then sweating. Grace cared for me selflessly: she slept by me even though I was coughing and sweating and vomiting through the night. She soaked cloths in warm water and wiped my face and neck down, her own face full of worry. When she wrapped three blankets around me and held me, I loved her more than ever. We decided not to go to the doctor because we had just spent all our money on the recruitment fee.

The other guys who had been recruited had left for the Gulf while I was sick. I was devastated. I thought at first that all our money was lost—the money our families had given us as a wedding present. I knew Grace's father would resent me for failing to fulfil the condition on which he had agreed to let me marry his daughter. For the first time, I yelled at Grace. I told her that she was a foolish girl, that she should have let me leave, sick or not, that her girlish doting had ruined our futures. I thought she would cry. Instead, she stared at me, her face impassive. I was struck by the terrifying thought that I barely knew my wife.

When I went into town to speak to the recruitment officer, Emmanuel, he said that, although he could not refund my fee, he would keep me on a waiting list. He could not say how long it would take. I went down to the recruitment office every day for two weeks, until Emmanuel found work for me. He charged me an additional fee for off-season enrolment. What could I do? If I did not pay, he would have sent another guy instead. I had to borrow money from Grace's father for the additional amount. In the end, all the recruitment fees cost more than two million shillings. After that, everything happened quickly. I didn't even know I was being sent to the UAE until after the papers were ready. Three days later, Grace, my parents, my sisters and Grace's parents came to see me off at Zanzibar International Airport.

The night before I left, Grace's mother cooked two whole fish in coconut and pilau, rice with spices. After dinner, Grace's father said that he was proud of me. 'It tells me that you are ready to be a man,' he pronounced, 'and only a man can take care of my daughter.'

When I said goodbye to Grace at the airport, I was relieved

to see her crying. She had been cold to me since I had yelled at her, although not so much that anyone else would notice. I hadn't been sure how we would leave things. It had been a big shift from dating to marriage. It was not about the sex. That was good. We could finally be in a bedroom instead of deserted parks or beaches, where she had always been uncomfortable and I worried she wasn't really enjoying herself. But I had never spent much time with Grace before, never seen her in the morning without make-up, never seen the blank expression she wore when she was doing chores, or how she was her father's favourite. I was also living away from home for the first time, in her family home: everyone had agreed it was best for her to stay there while I was working in the Gulf.

At the departure gate, Grace pressed her face against my chest, sobbing as I held the back of her head and squeezed her thick, long hair. I wondered what our marriage would be like when I came back. Then I had to go.

Standing on the tarmac in Abu Dhabi and hearing the *adhan*, the call to prayer, for the first time in a new place, I felt like a stranger. The land was wide and empty and hot. In Zanzibar, the morning *adhan* was always peaceful, dark blue still hanging in the sky, and somewhere in the house was the sound of a woman awake, filing pots and jugs with water. That first morning in Abu Dhabi, the *adhan* sounded indifferent. The notes were musical, but they seemed abbreviated, and the deep timbre of the singing shocked me. It was like hearing the voice of a strange man in your own house.

A shuttle was waiting to take me to ICAD, the Industrial

City of Abu Dhabi accommodation facility for migrant workers in the suburb of Mussafah, a fifty-minute ride from the university where I would work. As we drove, I stared out at the cream-and-pink brick houses, some of them beautiful mansions with curved outlines. The streets were wide and clean, almost empty of people. I felt as if I was looking into somebody's empty house while they were away, or walking around a school when the students had left for the summer holidays. Abu Dhabi was beautiful, and more so the longer I stayed there, but it always had that eerie, unreal quality.

At ICAD, four storeys of grey concrete, inside and out, they were not expecting me yet, so I was given temporary accommodation for a few weeks in an empty block. Each room had four bunk beds wrapped in faded green-and-white-checked sheets. We had to keep the place spotless for monthly maintenance inspections. As we were reassigned every semester, no one bothered to decorate. There was a communal bathroom at the end of the hall, and a kitchen and lounge on the second floor. I had a restless first night in my empty room, unable to imagine what life would bring next.

In the morning, I caught the shuttle bus to the university with other ICAD workers. There seemed to be nothing but highway and orange sand. Then a majestic, stark-white, domed building rose from the horizon. It was the most beautiful place I had ever seen. The main entrance—which workers didn't use—was a courtyard full of palm trees that reached as high as the sixth storey. The campus consisted of many separate buildings, most of which I would never go to, joined by an outdoor walkway along the length of the third storey. All the windows were gleaming.

I was assigned to work in the cafeteria, clearing away and washing dishes. Work was erratic in the first week because I didn't have my ID yet and they didn't have me on the roster sheet for entering the university or taking the shuttle bus. They did not seem to have my name anywhere. When my supervisor, Adnan, told me to take a break and report to the Workers Affairs office, I thought the university did not need me anymore. Often during my first year in Abu Dhabi, I caught myself suspecting that I was not really supposed to be there. But it turned out they just had to arrange an orientation for me and a handful of other workers who had also arrived off-season.

I had a lot of trouble with my recruitment fee and was often in the Workers Affairs office, where a woman named Farah told me she needed my recruitment fee receipt in order to reimburse me for the fees I had paid in Zanzibar—nine hundred and eighty US dollars. I didn't know that I needed a receipt. I couldn't remember if Emmanuel had given me a receipt. He had told me that my recruitment fee was all in the paperwork he had sent to my employer, but Farah had no record of it. I was very upset: it was so much money and I was supposed to be sending money home to my family and to Grace as soon as possible. Farah explained that Emmanuel's recruitment office would have sent my paperwork to an official recruiting company, which would have sent it to a company in the UAE called ADAC. They would have sent it to one of their smaller branches, one of which was called RECO, the hospitality company that assigned workers to the university.

Farah said that my receipt had probably got lost somewhere along the way, either at ADAC or RECO, or perhaps the Tanzanian government or the UAE government had to approve my application first. In any case, Emmanuel should have given it to me to bring to my new place of work. Back at ICAD, I looked through all my papers to check if I had the receipt. I had tried to be as organised as possible, but I didn't understand a lot of the papers. There was no receipt. I returned to Workers Affairs at least five times, but I never got my reimbursement. There was nothing to be done, and I suppose it was nobody's fault but my own.

The stress of earning back the recruitment fee stayed with me through my first year in Abu Dhabi. I didn't make friends straightaway. There weren't many Africans working at the university. Most of the other workers were Filipinos and Indians; I got along well with the Indians in particular. Some of them were security guards, because they had good English, like Abdul, one of my roommates. Many of the workers assigned to the cafeteria or to my section in ICAD had arrived just a few months before me. We mostly kept to ourselves in the first year, all under a lot of pressure to send money home. I spent my evenings messaging my family. The wifi in ICAD wasn't strong enough to make calls. The ICAD manager told us later that apps like Facebook and Skype were not permitted for calls in the UAE, that we had to use an Etisalat international calling card. Only Abdul bought the cards, to call his mother, until she yelled at him for wasting money instead of sending it home.

Grace was very sweet in her messages to me. I didn't know if her recent coldness had disappeared or if it just wasn't communicated over messages. In the beginning, her words were comforting, but they became repetitive. Sometimes, when she was texting, I couldn't confidently match up her words with the way I remembered her. My sisters messaged me photos of home, and then eventually there wasn't much to say, and they stopped.

My friendship with Abdul started a few months into my first year, one Saturday when he asked me if I wanted to buy KFC with him and some of the other Indian guys. He said he would kill himself if he ate another bite of ICAD food—watery, bland daal and a stiff bread roll. I hesitated. I was always calculating how much money I had and how much I could send home. But I wanted a friend. I gave Abdul twenty dirhams. The Indian guys went out and brought back bags of fried chicken. We ate in the lounge. It was the best food I'd had since leaving Zanzibar and probably the best moment of my first year.

I found out that many of the Indian guys did not have receipts for the reimbursement fees either, but that most of the Filipinos did. Apparently, the Filipinos were not playing fair. A lot of them were supervisors and managers in the cafeteria and gave other Filipino workers better break times and more overtime shifts. They also got the African and Indian guys to carry heavier things and do the tougher jobs, and talked and joked more with the students, which meant the queues were longer and the dishes piled up. Abdul also told me that Filipino security guards got to work inside and put the Indians and the African guys outside, where it is always so hot. At ICAD, the Filipinos were always the loudest, especially at night, when the security guards got back at odd hours and sang loudly in Tagalog in the common area.

Soon I was back at Workers Affairs to talk about my passport. I had handed it over when I arrived and had been waiting almost a year to get it back. The job contract stipulated that the university would pay for one return flight home per year. It was time for my trip, but I still did not have my passport. When they had sent us forms to register for our annual trip home and asked for our passports, I could not fill out the form. Another woman in Workers Affairs, Ashley, told me the university did not have it, that RECO was holding it for processing, so she had to wait to talk to them. I came back the following week and she said that RECO could not return my passport yet—it was still being processed with the government. RECO said that I should have formally requested the return of my passport months ago if I needed it now. Ashley could see how upset I was. She said she would flag my case as a 'Level Four' case and Workers Affairs would prioritise it. I sat in a conference room with Ashley and Farah while they sorted through my files and filled out forms to make an expedited request to RECO. But when I came back the next week, they told me nothing could be done. My passport was still with the government, and there was no possibility of me getting home for my annual leave. They assured me that I could still keep my room in ICAD for the summer months and that they would get RECO to provide a food stipend until I returned to work. But I would have to stay in Abu Dhabi for the summer. Three months.

I had been counting on going home, and had made plans with Grace and my family. Instead, I watched at the end of the semester while everyone else got ready to leave Abu Dhabi. All the chatter in ICAD was about gifts for relatives and the food everyone was going to eat back home in Pakistan, Bangladesh, India, the Philippines or and Ethiopia. I could see the excitement among the students too. They passed the cafeteria on their way out to the main entrance, where taxis left for the airport. Dressed in track pants and hoodies and dragging large suitcases, they hugged and laughed and cried as they said goodbye to friends.

I still did not really have a friend here. Abdul and I had grown apart. His preparations for home had continued for almost a month. He said he was sorry for me when I found out my passport was held up, but he forgot about it soon enough. Then he showed me an Arab perfume containing oud oil that he had bought to take home for his wife. He went on to talk about how he couldn't wait to have sex with her again. Although we used to talk about sex often, I got angry and said he was perverted. After that he stayed out of my way.

Abu Dhabi was especially empty in the summer because it was the season of Ramadan. Before Ramadan began, I caught the bus to the Corniche, the long artificial beach beside the city. I had heard that the white and yellow sand was imported from abroad, from places as far away as Australia. I took off my sneakers, but the sand was so hot that I had to sit down. White tourists lay on beach towels in bikinis. Emirati couples and families walked across the sand, the women in black burkas and hijabs and the men in long white kanduras and ghutra headscarves. Gleaming blue skyscrapers lined the pale-yellow length of the Corniche. Disoriented, I wandered around downtown Abu Dhabi, imagining Grace there with me, and the comments we would make about what we saw. But I wasn't sure I was imagining her correctly.

Although I had been working in Abu Dhabi for a year, I knew so little of the city. I felt as if I did not have permission to be there, to waste time there. It was nothing more than a workplace, and I was just waiting to get home to Zanzibar.

That first day downtown, I went inside a juice shop. A welcome blast of air conditioning hit me as I pushed on the heavy glass door. Inside, there was just enough room for two tables. The owner took my order from behind a glass pane he had filled with oranges and lemons. I asked for a papaya-and-banana juice. The papaya was not nearly as sweet as the papaya at home, but it was still good. When three Emirati men came in, I left to give them my table.

I stayed on the street for a while, finishing my juice. From across the street, I watched Emiratis take off their leather sandals before entering a small mosque opposite. The evening call to prayer is my favourite. Although the deep voice and the Arabic still made me feel like a stranger, it was undeniably calming. The skies were smeared with soft pink and orange and fathers were steering their children into the mosque by the shoulders. The soft fabric of the women's burkas swayed as they followed.

Even though my family, and everyone I know in Zanzibar, were Muslim, I had never prayed five times a day, or even daily. There was a men's prayer room in ICAD. It was a small space, about two by two metres, a simple red rug on the stone floor, no windows. I had only glanced in there when I first arrived at ICAD. That summer I went in every day. It was always empty. I knelt, and didn't know what else to do at first. I was tired of my own thoughts. But then I started to picture places in Zanzibar, as though testing myself to remember them properly. My parents' house appeared vividly to me. I knew how many steps I took to walk from one end of each room to the other, and how far I could run my hand along the mantelpiece in our living room before reaching the edge, and how much dust was there, depending on the week of the month. And how low I had to duck to get under the curtain my sisters had put up to divide their shared bedroom.

I could see the picture frames my mother liked so much: thick, gold-painted wood with rose designs, framing photos of our distant relatives from various branches of the family, not photos of our immediate family. The living-room walls were covered with my father's tattered posters of Zanzibari and Tanzanian figures and events. There was a poster of Sheikh Abdullah Saleh Farsy, the Zanzibari poet and Islamic scholar, and a handful of promotional posters of the Zanzibar

International Film Festival, even though my father had read none of the Sheikh's writing and seen none of the films. Neema's patterned cloths covered every flat surface, along with Sophy's cut-outs of Nigerian movie stars, and Mary's and Faith's figurines. These items and decorations would have changed slightly while I was away. An old poster would have been replaced by a more recent film-festival poster. New baby photos would be squeezed into the edges of old frames.

I went downtown two more times, once to have shawarma, thin slices of chicken shaved off a glistening spit and wrapped in pita with fries, onions, tomatoes and thoom, a light garlic paste. The second time I had dosa, a crispy Indian pancake filled with spiced potatoes. The Indian cook watched me from behind a perspex pane, from which an arch had been cut out for transactions. He was standing up straight, his head leaning back, as though to take in as much of the scene as possible.

'Where are you from?' he asked.

'Zanzibar,' I said, and he nodded authoritatively. I thought it was unlikely he knew where it was. Most of the Indian guys at ICAD had not heard of Zanzibar before meeting me.

'Where do you work?' he continued after a while.

I was trying to finish the dosa as quickly as possible, but the potatoes were too hot to scoff. I told him about the university, but he didn't know where it was.

'Construction?' he asked.

'No. Waiter.'

'Your first time?' he asked after another pause. I didn't

know what he meant. He pointed to my plate. 'The dosa,' he said.

I nodded.

'You like it?'

'It's good, very good.'

He smiled contentedly and kept watching me.

'Good, good. You will come back, huh?'

I nodded as I chewed, then I scooped up the last of the chutney and got up to leave.

'You are not tall like the other Africans.' He chuckled. 'Some of them are *big* and *tall*.' He stretched out his arms to demonstrate. 'A lot of Africans in the NBA.'

I laughed half-heartedly.

'You will come back, yes? Bring your friends. The ones who work at the new university.'

'I will,' I said.

I was about to leave, but went to the counter instead. 'Where are you from in India? One of my friends here is from Mumbai.'

'Me too, I am from Mumbai.'

'You too?'

'There are a lot of people from Mumbai, *beta*,' he laughed. 'Twenty million of us.'

'There are a lot of foreign workers in Abu Dhabi.'

'Yes. We *are* the city. Everything works here because of us,' he said loudly, and slapped a dough-dusted palm on the counter. 'Don't you know, eighty per cent of Abu Dhabi is foreign workers.'

He told me that his name was Arjun. He was thirty-six. He had been working in Abu Dhabi for six years and had four children back home in Mumbai. His favourite was his son Aditya, thirteen years old and incredibly smart. Arjun hoped Aditya could go to school in America or the UK. Every year Arjun saved enough money to buy Abu Dhabi gold for his wife, who claimed it was the best gold in the world.

I smiled and laughed as he spoke, making sure he felt at ease. It wasn't how I used to behave at home. In Abu Dhabi, I felt older, different. I thought of myself standing there in a downtown dosa shop speaking to an Indian cook. I could have been anyone. It was like the feeling I had on the tarmac when I first landed in Abu Dhabi, as if I could start walking in any direction and no one would know I was gone, but this time I was okay. I told Arjun that I would come back with Abdul after the summer.

Once Ramadan began, all the shops were closed during the day. A few food places remained open behind blackout blinds, but you could only buy takeaway. It was too hot to be downtown anyway, sometimes forty-one or forty-two degrees. I took the bus down once, but it was so miserable I waited for the next bus back. With even fewer people on the street, Abu Dhabi looked like a city inside a snowdome, encased in a bubble of heat. The searing light reflected from the surface of the skyscrapers bounced inside the globe.

I began to spend hours at a time lying in bed, the fan pointed towards me, unhappy, drowsy, not speaking to anyone, sometimes for days. I was sweating all the time. I went to the prayer room just for somewhere to go. As I knelt, thick beads of sweat dripped down my chest. I closed my eyes and pictured the Zanzibar beaches, the cool water, the veiny lines of sunlight dancing on the surface, the rustling of the beaded bracelets sold by old men and women to tourists on the beach, and the drenching rain we would get after a whole week of sun. It had not rained once in Abu Dhabi since I had been there. The heat was so much drier than hot days in Zanzibar. I began to lose weight because I didn't feel like eating. With my food stipend from RECO, I got myself bread, ham, oranges and biscuits from the grocery store in Mussafah, but I hardly touched any of it.

One afternoon an ICAD manager told me to go to a meeting at Workers Affairs. I was so thankful to have to be somewhere again. Perhaps my passport had finally returned? There were still almost two months left of summer and enough time to arrange to go home. But my hopes were dashed: Ashley told me that RECO needed more waiters on one of their other projects, a three-day international conference at a hotel. I immediately accepted.

Two days later, I caught an early bus with twelve other ICAD workers. The hotel was even bigger than the university campus. Thick, blue marble lettering greeted us at the entrance, before we followed a winding path, lined with topiaried shrubs, which led to a cluster of ornate, cream-and-blue private villas facing the beach, some with their own tennis court. The bus continued, via an underground carpark, to the workers' entrance. We collected our uniforms and I was assigned to the kitchen. One of the hotel restaurants served as an all-day buffet. They needed me at the roast-beef station.

The hotel was like a palace. My restaurant was round and cavernous, with white walls and high ceilings, and looked onto dense foliage—through the fronds you could see blue-green seawater, a sparkling pool, tiles tessellating in brilliant dark and light blues, and lounges made of cream canvas. The air conditioning maintained the room at a perfect temperature. The conference attendees were poised and well-dressed, the men in light-coloured suits and the women sporting colourful silk scarves. Everyone wore a lanyard displaying the conference logo—a blue-and-green globe circled by bare arms. As soon as I stepped out of the kitchen, I could smell the scent of the hotel, a fragrance that added to the dreamlike feeling of the place. It was subtle, neither floral nor fruity, neither musk nor oud. It was like a nut, both faint and sharp, as though you were standing in the field on which the nut was grown and caught the aroma of baking sugar, carried by the breeze. The other workers told me that the scent was pumped through the air conditioning, throughout the hotel.

It was easy work, and, even though the skin of my hands was scorched under the heat lamp all day as I carved beef (there was no sign of Ramadan inside the hotel), I couldn't drink in enough of the atmosphere of beauty and sophistication. There was also a dessert buffet, where the chefs varied the heights of the different desserts: entire iced cakes on platforms, towers of bite-sized tarts, shot glasses of mousses, and skewers of multicoloured fruit. I liked listening to the clinks of cups, forks, and spoons, and the gentle cadences of the academics' voices. I spoke brightly to all the guests. Some asked me about Zanzibar and I told them about the beautiful beaches and the mshikaki, the skewers of grilled mutton and goat sold on the street late at night. They said they would have to visit.

I was looking inside extreme Abu Dhabi luxury, only the surfaces of which I had glimpsed: the blue, glass skyscrapers, the sprawling five-star resorts, and the Emirates Palace, sitting at the other end of the Corniche, overlooking a field of fountains that glittered at night. I felt as if I was veering back and forth between two equally dreamlike places: from the hot, depressing stupor of my bed in ICAD at night, to the immaculately cool, glossy paradise of the hotel in the day.

When I returned my blue uniform at the end of the third day and took the bus back to ICAD from the hotel for the last time, I felt oppressed with fear, desperate not to live through the next seven or so hours until I could sleep. I was more desperate now than when I first found out that my passport had been withheld and I couldn't go home.

The next seven weeks passed in a blur of misery. I woke up late, weak from thirst, often snapping out of nightmares about the sickly, thick heat and the sweat that soaked through my shirt and sheets. I napped throughout the day, drifting in and out of sleep. I was sick of being awake, my thoughts spinning. I felt inexplicably estranged from Grace, Neema and my parents. I was so lonely that I had begun to message people who were not even close to me back home, and cousins I barely spoke to. But once we had got through some preliminary greetings, I couldn't bring myself to tell anyone how I was struggling. Relief came only when it was dark enough outside—it took too long in summer—and I could go to sleep again.

After weeks like this, there came a day when I simply could not get out of bed. I lay there, petrified and sweating. When I finally managed to stand up, after five hours, it was as though the volume in my body switched on and I could hear my heart beating, booming between my ears. I ran to the bathroom to splash water on my face, and looked in the mirror, afraid there was something wrong with me. I headed to the prayer room, where I wished for the health and happiness of each member of my family, trying to calm myself by picturing their faces and voices. Then I went outside the ICAD compound, pacing as I waited for the cool of the evening, before forcing myself to do push-ups and stretches, trying to feel stronger. Before the summer ended, I experienced two similar episodes.

When Abdul and the other workers returned and asked how my summer had been, I told them, as though it was a fun story, about the absurd beauty and luxury of the hotel. It was all I could offer to match their stories of their homes, wives, girlfriends and families. I was so thankful for their chatter that I treated them more warmly than before and spoke to them for as long as I could. When I was stationed back at the sandwich bar, I asked students about their summer travels and, if they asked, I told them about Zanzibar.

One afternoon, when I was making a grilled vegetable wrap

for a tall student from Canada, I asked him why he seemed worried. He told me about assignments that were due soon, how his applications for internships had been rejected, and that he was late turning in a budget for the student body. His breathlessness reminded me of my mother, who became anxious and flustered whenever there was a problem with finances at the beef business. I remembered the calm, smiling manner with which Neema comforted our mother.

'*Pole pole*,' I said to him.

'*Pole*—what is that?'

'It's Swahili. It means *slowly, gently*,' I tried to smile the way Neema did—with patience, kindness—and I thought I could see his expression relax. 'Take it slowly.'

I became popular with the students, so Adnan gave me more shifts on the sandwich bar. That's how I became friends with Ricky, a Filipino guy who had been on the main sandwich bar before I arrived. Ricky treated me like an old friend. He told me gossip about the workers—about their salaries, their romances, and we compared our favourite students and professors. Ricky opened up a social world in ICAD and on campus that made my life seem more real. The Filipinos treated Abu Dhabi like their home. I came to like their loud and cheerful manner, which had annoyed me earlier. I began to act in the same way.

The second year in Abu Dhabi passed more easily. My passport was returned to Workers Affairs. Farah explained that the long wait was not routine, that there had been a problem with RECO's processing. She said that Workers

Affairs would now hold my passport for me, because of the *kafala* law in the Gulf that required employers to hold migrant workers' passports, but it would be accessible to me whenever I needed it. Because of my case, and others like mine, Workers Affairs would transition into directly handling the passport processing for new full-time workers of the university, rather than leaving it to contractors like RECO. Farah asked me to sign a form saying that I understood and agreed to everything about my passport. I thought she might have been taking precautions because of the rumours about migrant workers trapped by employers, like the maids in Oman whose passports were withheld. But I trusted Farah and the other women in Workers Affairs. I signed, and there were no further problems with my passport.

Abdul told me that the rumours were true—in the UAE there were a lot of workers whose passports were confiscated, who tried to leave their employer because of horrible working conditions and accommodation, but who could not. He knew Indians and Bangladeshi construction workers who lived in apartments with ten or even fifteen men to a small bedroom, in places so old and dirty there were rats and you could get sick just from sleeping there. They were forced to work overtime in the sun even during the summer—'The newspapers in Mumbai are full of these stories, *full* of them!' said Abdul. He told me that the police had once arrested workers at their accommodation, beaten them and deported them because they had gone on strike, which was illegal in the UAE.

'It's not supposed to be like this. It is not allowed to happen like this,' he said, tucking his bedsheet in neatly one morning, 'but sometimes it does. You don't know how lucky we are to work for the university.'

'Have you ever met these men?' I asked.

'No, but I've seen them. Some came to the university for construction jobs. Only for a few weeks—short-term contract, right? But when the university found out the problems with their usual employer or contractor, and with their accommodation, they were taken off the job. Just like that. It would have been the best-paying job they ever had in this country, too,' he spat. 'Poor guys. These guys who look just like me.'

We were in the communal ICAD bathroom, brushing our teeth. I was about to ask why they came here in the first place, but stopped myself. It was a foolish question. Everyone in ICAD knows the answer: because it is worse at home.

Abdul glanced at my reflection in the mirror. His expression changed to one of annoyance.

'It's no good talking about that. Things are very good for us here now.'

On the bus rides between Mussafah and the island, I sometimes looked at the construction sites and thought about the Abu Dhabi I didn't know. But mostly I didn't want to think about it. The university was taking care of us. They finished building a workers' recreation space on campus, with a small kitchen, couches and a pool table. I didn't spend much time there because my break was only half an hour, and I stayed in the cafeteria to eat. Security guards used the space between shifts to nap. Later, it was where Workers Affairs held information sessions about how to raise complaints or provide feedback anonymously. Workers were required to go to at least one session, but could attend up to three. We liked the sessions because we were paid for the full hour and they had a beverage table, the kind I usually prepared for student or guest events: two tables with a black cloth, tea, coffee and biscuits. Workers Affairs also held another mandatory session about journalists—to inform us that we were to contact Workers Affairs before speaking to any journalists who approached us. But no one I knew was ever approached by a journalist.

By the end of my second year, I was eligible for a pay increase. I had finally paid off my recruitment fees, I was sending more money home and I had more money to spend in Abu Dhabi on my days off. I couldn't join in fully with Abdul's Indian friends and with Ricky's Filipino friends because I didn't speak their languages, but they often included me. I took Abdul to the dosa place where I had eaten during the summer, and I went with Ricky and his friends to Filipino restaurants in Mussafah and downtown. Some nights we watched movies in ICAD. The night we watched *Fast and Furious 7*, the room cheered when the car jumped between the two Etihad Towers. I recognised the towers from my trips to the Corniche and felt proud of Abu Dhabi.

In January, the coolest month, university life slowed down while the students were studying abroad. We were given a long weekend off, with full pay, and I pitched in with Abdul and his friends to buy cricket equipment, ten dirhams each. For three days, we played in the car park out the front of ICAD. On the last day, Indians vs Sri Lankans, the losers (Indians) bought KFC for everyone to share. It kept me out of my own head and I didn't feel anything like the drowsiness of summer. I was still going to the prayer room every day. I felt self-conscious about it because I didn't know much about Islam, not like the other Muslim guys who came to pray. But I kept doing what I had started in the summer: closing my eyes and remembering as much as I could of home, scene by scene.

Finally, six months later, I was back at Abu Dhabi airport, on my way home for the summer break. It was oppressively hot again, just like when I first stepped out of the airport almost three years ago. This time I was coming back to the airport with a bus load of other ICAD workers, some of them new friends. My carry-on bag jangled, full of magnets, keychains and photo frames, and heavy with five kilos of medjool dates. In my suitcase were five different perfumes that Abdul had helped me choose for Grace and my sisters. My favourite was for Grace; I would let my sisters choose among the other four. I smiled, imagining how my sisters would argue over them, and complain that Grace had got the most expensive perfume. I hugged the other workers when we parted for our different gates. I was not close to them—Abdul and Ricky were flying out on other days—but we were all feeling excited at the prospect of being home soon. Even the twinge of knowing I would miss Abu Dhabi over the next two months made me elated: it meant that I was looking forward to coming back.

On the plane, everything slowed down, but I felt fine. I was in my best polo shirt, a yellow one that I knew Grace liked, and I had on new sandals I had bought in Abu Dhabi earlier that year. I had shaved carefully that morning. A lot of people were coming to Zanzibar airport to pick me up. Neema told me that she had arranged a minibus to take everybody to and from the airport. I imagined stepping through the gate in Zanzibar, proud and confident, like other Zanzibaris coming back from overseas. I had changed, and I wondered how soon my family would notice. I think I was more handsome. I had lost weight and my jaw was more defined. I had outgrown the soft, babyish face I used to have. When I thought about my old name, Fredy Mpole, I was no longer irritated: I had only been that sensitive boy for a short time, and his embarrassments seemed minor now. The people at ICAD saw me, I think, as somewhat pensive, but mostly easygoing, and willing to join in. And now I had Neema's smile. I wanted to be that person for the people at home. I felt like that person.

Aunts and uncles at the Mwanakwerekwe market would ask me what Abu Dhabi was like. Would I recommend it for their sons? Staring out at the cream-coloured rooftops as my plane took off, I asked myself: how could I begin to describe my experience? Ricky had given me a photo as a goodbye present: Ricky and me grinning behind the sandwich bar. One of Ricky's favourite students had taken it. I slid it into a photo frame I had bought for my mother. The cafeteria looked fancy in the photo: shiny, dark wood panels, a brick feature wall, and *Marhaba*, the word for welcome, in large Arabic and Roman letters mounted on the wall behind us, lit up in bright purple. I was brandishing a baguette and Ricky was shaking a bottle of pesto, the students' favourite sauce.

I didn't know how much of Abu Dhabi I wanted to describe, or even if I would be able to describe it. I could tell them about the heat, the university, the students, the palaces, the fragrance and the glossy tiles of the hotel. I could tell them about cricket and KFC on long weekends. I would warn them to keep receipts for recruitment fees. I could say that I was praying every day now. And some things I would keep to myself.

Before the Lights Go Out

After the exhibition was taken down, people asked me how it felt to be an artist. They always said the word in English. Buwa, my father, couldn't say it without laughing. He had heard what I was saying to my friends at the university: *It was a real honour to show people how the civil war hurt us Nepalese, it was an emotional experience,* etc.

Buwa stared down over his white moustache and smacked me on the head. He had always done this, teasing for the most part.

'Forget it, Buwa,' I told him, and his laugh turned into a sneer.

The exhibition closed after three months because there was no custodian for the space. Not long afterwards, we received a magazine from Julie in America. Manna, our maid, brought it to me at breakfast. She had already torn open the plastic sleeve and riffled through the magazine.

'You are famous, Mister Artist,' said Manna. She opened the magazine to the page with my photo, the one I used for the exhibition, and pointed to my name in small print underneath: Ngodup Thapa.

Manna handed me the small yellow card that had come with the package and I moved over to the window to read it. Printed in serif font, the card read: *Congratulations, it is important to show how the civil war hurt your people; it is a very emotional image.* Julie's signature was printed at the bottom. The card had curly lines, like English vines, embossed around the borders. I started to itch.

Julie first visited our house in Balkot earlier this year, one day in March, in the evening before the electricity went out. I could see her approaching our house with her driver. I changed my shirt before I went to open the door.

'We have a guest,' I called out to Buwa. 'A white woman.'

He was in the study, measuring our chairs for new cushion covers.

'What, at this time?'

Julie had come in a taxi organised by the university; her driver was a local Nepalese man. He came to the door with her and gushed about her art career in New York. I went to find Manna before she left for the day and asked her to make us some chai.

'What, at this time?' Manna said.

'Yes,' I said. 'We will be waiting in the living room.'

'You think you can take an American lady to the living room in the state it's in?' She sent me to make the chai while she pulled the old cushions out of the cupboard.

Years ago, the living room was where Buwa talked to professors and activists about the state of affairs with the war. The furnishings had once included cabinets full of old books and keepsakes, and a red rug with a gold trim, which Aama, my mother, had ordered from India. Since her death seven years ago, Buwa had removed the decorations one by one. The professors and activists had stopped coming.

I heaped four spoonfuls of sugar into each cup and carried the tray up the steps into the living room. Julie was sitting cross-legged. The cushions had faded. I watched Julie move her knee to hide a dark stain on the rug. She was dressed all in white. Her sand-coloured hair was short and wavy, and I found myself following the arc of wisps that fell onto her face. At that moment, I thought she was the most beautiful woman I had ever seen. She looked up at me.

'I love your photographs, Ngodup,' she said.

I sat down, as still as possible, unsure how to answer.

'What photos? I didn't know you were taking photos,' said Buwa.

'They were for a university class,' I said.

'Your professor gave them to me. I think you reveal the

true face of the civil war,' said Julie.

'Thank you.'

'Your photographs would be a great addition to the event I'm creating, about the horror of Nepal's civil war as seen through the eyes of the locals,' she said. 'We've got a really great space near Kathmandu. We're hoping to keep the house as a museum after the event.'

'The old Maharjan house?' Buwa asked.

'Yes, exactly.' Julie smiled.

I was surprised he knew anything about it.

'What does my son have to do for the show?' said Buwa. He was in a new linen shirt, his arms stretched out straight, holding his knees.

'It's not a show,' said Julie. 'It's a space featuring some works.'

'An exhibition,' said Buwa.

'Yes, a space for art.'

She reached for her cup. Her rings clinked against the china. I recognised them from the stalls by Durbar Square, copper bands with coloured glass, five hundred rupees apiece.

'What do you think, Ngodup?' she asked. 'Can I use your work?'

I glanced at Buwa.

'We would only display one image,' said Julie. 'There's one that stands out. The portrait.'

She smiled and I looked away to stop myself staring at her. I didn't know which one she meant.

'I'm thinking about calling it *Woman*,' Julie said. 'I think it says a lot about gender and female pain.'

I avoided Buwa's eyes.

'Do you want to do this, Ngodup?' Buwa asked.

Julie looked startled. But perhaps it was only the colour of her eyes, so clear and blue.

'Yes. Of course.'

When she was leaving, I accompanied Julie from the living room. Up close, her hair was so fine I could see her scalp, pale and glistening. Her blouse fluttered as she dropped down a step and yelped.

The next day, I was driving into Kathmandu with my girl-friend, Shabnam, behind me on the bike, her crotch pushed against my back. I was thinking about Julie, and the way her blouse floated around her and how you'd have to catch her inside it.

I turned and said to Shabnam, 'I'll show you a secret road.'

The bike leaned to the right when Shabnam reached down for her shoe. She had been fiddling with it since we had entered the gravel road.

'Stop it!' I shouted.

I stuck out my foot to realign the bike and a shooting pain went through my knee. The bike was so much heavier with Shabnam on it. Her hair brushed against a branch as I veered onto the side road off Hattisar Sadak. It was tight but I had to go fast.

We were looking at the facade of Hotel Yak and Yeti, the hundred-year-old palace from the Rana dynasty that had been turned into a five-star hotel. The pink-and-white structure was only five storeys tall, but encompassed the grand courtyard inside.

'The American woman, Julie, is staying here,' I told Shabnam.

All the lights were blazing. In Kathmandu, the electricity went off at night, except at hotels rated four stars and above. I wanted to watch for longer, but it wasn't as fun being there with Shabnam as I'd thought it would be.

'The Shangri-La is nicer,' she said.

I knew she was jealous. Neither of us had stayed at either the Yak and Yeti or the Shangri-La. We turned the bike around and drove for another half an hour back to Balkot.

At the edge of town, I stopped the bike on an empty road, grass fields on either side. I didn't have to catch Shabnam, whose pink shirt stuck to her stomach and peeled off easily. The grass was dry and prickled when I leaned over. Her lipstick was bright pink. Her body beneath me, I stared out at the bike parked nearby. In the dark, everything lay low and lumpy: the rubbish piled along the bank of a creek in the distance, the rubble on the road, and the unfinished cement houses, all without lights. Even when I was inside her I felt as if I could just get up and walk away.

Shabnam didn't say a word. I had to ask her what was wrong and she seemed to relish taking her time to answer.

'You know you're never going to be better than this,' she said, giving me a dirty look.

I thought of the different things I could do: hit her, drive away and leave her there, or tell her that she didn't know what she was talking about, that I didn't care about the art.

'That's not what this is about,' I said, and then drove her home.

On the morning of the opening, Manna stood behind me as I looked in the mirror. She fiddled with the sleeves of my shirt, making it bag around my arms. The skin on my forehead was dark and shiny and a new pimple was erupting on my chin.

'You used too much gel on my hair!' I shouted, swatting her away.

'Don't you talk to me like that,' Manna growled, combing the hair off my forehead.

Everybody knew about Julie and the exhibition. In conversations, I secretly waited for someone to bring it up and they always did. The art and journalism students had been asking to swap work with me. Buwa, however, had commented that Julie had a nicer house for her exhibition than he had for his children, even though I was his only child and our house was bigger. Manna complained that Julie was too skinny and her hair was too short, like a boy's.

There were a lot of white people at the opening, including students from Trinity International College and a university in Abu Dhabi. Buwa had said he would come, but I hadn't seen him yet. Julie stood up and welcomed a foreign photographer, whose work had been printed in *National Geographic*. Then she paused and lowered her gaze.

'The Nepalese Civil War was a war wreaked on civilians. Seventeen thousand, eight hundred people died.' Her voice was so calm it was almost sinister. She had on a new set of rings. 'As we gather the stories of rebels and local people, we begin to give power back to the civilians of Nepal. There is power in taking control of our narratives.'

Her smooth, American-accented English was so different from ours. After the applause, Julie took the foreign photographer around the exhibition.

Most of the pictures were of bloodied bodies on the battlefield. I felt no real connection to them. All I knew of the war, which had ended five years ago, in 2006, were the long years of discussion: ageing activists studying constitutions, harassed journalists posing dead-end questions, sweaty professors shouting through slideshows, living rooms dense with the musk of frustrated old men and smoky chai. Buwa was once excited for me to study politics. But by the time I was old enough for university, he had already shut out the war, and it became easy for me to ignore it too. I had grown sick of talks about what Nepal was, who the Nepalese people were, what communism was and what democracy was. I didn't feel certain about any of those things the way my classmates seemed to be. So Buwa and I abided by the curfews in the final year of the war and waited out the protests from our house in Balkot, arranging and rearranging the furniture. I wondered if Julie knew I had never been at a protest or on a battlefield. I had never even seen someone die.

My photograph was of Aakar's mother crying at his burial. Aakar, a friend of my friend from university, died in the Badarmude bus explosion. As I walked towards the photograph on the wall, I imagined his mother's eyes boring into me, and I was filled with dread. What if Aakar's mother, or somebody who knew her, came to the exhibition?

I stared at the image of her sagging dark skin, her sharp chin and her large, sad eyes. She had not noticed when I'd trained the lens on her, which made it a better photograph than the other ones I had taken. Her face filled the whole frame. Her mouth was downturned and tears pooled in a deep crease on her left cheek.

I felt a hand on my back and knew it was Julie's.

'Ngodup. You should be proud,' she said earnestly.

It struck me suddenly how far she had travelled to be here and how different her real life must be.

'What do you like about it?' I asked.

She had that startled look again. She turned to the photo.

'It's so full of life,' she said.

'What do you mean?'

As if in slow motion, the foreign photographer approached Julie and touched her on the back as she had done to me.

'I'll be right back,' she said, smiling brightly.

I went around the exhibition by myself, avoiding the other university students. I looped through the exhibition another three times, but Julie was always busy.

When I got home, Buwa had a pamphlet from the exhibition on the coffee table in front of him. For a moment, I was offended that he had not spoken to me there.

'What did you say to her?' Buwa said.

'Who?'

'Aakar's mother, when you were at his burial.'

'I didn't talk to her there.'

'Did you ask her if you could use her photograph in the exhibition?' he asked.

'She doesn't know I took it.'

He stared at me and I thought he looked very old.

'You took photographs about the *war*?' His voice rose as though he were about to yell.

I didn't reply, waiting for him to continue, but eventually he just hiccupped and left the room.

I went to bed feeling as if no one was talking about the same thing, but that perhaps my photograph was good because at least it made people feel something. That night, little lumps appeared on the inside of my thighs.

Julie didn't sleep with me. She slept with Paresh, another university student, and then she went back to America. Paresh was five years older than me and studying economics. He was not particularly handsome, rich or smart. No one mentioned the photograph again once Julie had left. Buwa was still barely speaking to me.

Every time I thought about Julie I felt anxious. One day at university, I asked Shabnam:

'If you had to describe me, what would you say?'

She was about to go into a lecture. She burst out laughing so hard she couldn't speak, but I knew she was faking it.

In between gulps, she said, 'That's not what this is about.' And then she went inside the classroom, laughing.

I stormed off.

The lumps on my thighs were growing bigger and more inflamed. They hurt when I climbed onto my bike or when my thighs rubbed against each other. I hadn't had sex with Shabnam for weeks, since the night we'd gone to watch the Hotel Yak and Yeti. All I could think about now was the caption under my photograph at the exhibition: *Tirtha Kumari Bhujel, widower and mother of three, grieves at her eldest son's funeral at Naubise village near Kathmandu.*

I planned to ask Buwa what was wrong, and tell him that I had apologised to Aakar's mother, although I had no intention of meeting her. The day I went to talk to him, he was on his knees in the study, measuring a chair for cushion covers again. I was sure he heard my footsteps approaching, but he didn't turn around. I walked away.

I was convinced I was getting sick in the same way Aama had. I didn't tell anyone, because she had died from a woman's disease, so that could not have been the case for me.

But I didn't die, and then it was the anniversary of Aama's death and my turn to clean the shrine. I woke up early and went out to Durbar Square to collect the bucket and scrubbing brush. The Buddhist shrine was off the main road and through a series of courtyards. Multicoloured prayer flags hung across the courtyard, strung between apartment windows. Several stories above them were clotheslines. I kneeled down and spread my thighs on either side of the Buddha's foot. It was cold from the morning dew and soothed my sores.

At noon, Widow Dhital, a friend of my father's, came down from her apartment to give me a bowl of *chiura*, beaten rice, and poured in *dahi*, a yogurt she made herself and kept in a large soft drink bottle. I still thought I was dying and I wanted to ask her about my sores, but she spoke first.

'Is your father getting better?'

I didn't know Buwa was sick. Perhaps Widow Dhital asked this about everyone's father, since the elders were always complaining about a cough or not sleeping well whenever there was a change in the weather. I chewed for a long time before speaking.

'He seems better,' I said finally.

When I had finished eating, she scraped the last wet flakes from my bowl and pinched my cheek.

'You know, Ngodup, I remember the way that your mother doted on you. It hasn't been the same since she died, has it?' she said.

I nodded. I didn't want to disagree with her.

Aama never doted on me. She was always scolding me, and often slapped me across the face when she was angry, not like the affectionate taps Buwa gave me on the head. For her, my marks were never high enough, and I was lazy and inconsiderate. Even when she was sick and in bed all day, she scolded me for leaving the house and not taking care of her, although Manna was there to attend to her every need. Buwa was the lenient one and covered for me when I went out, especially if I said it was for a protest. I avoided being at home, as Aama grew more irritable the sicker she became. She died in the night while I was out with my friends. I came back to find Buwa on the floor beside her bed, crying. His left leg was stuck out at a strange angle and his eyes were swollen. I had never seen Buwa look so weak and didn't wanted to embarrass him, so I didn't say anything.

'Buwa still misses her,' I told Widow Dhital.

And I suddenly missed him, even though I had just glimpsed him in the dining room this morning, eating breakfast alone.

The courtyard was full of people for Aama's anniversary ceremony. Relatives, friends and neighbours came to lay candles on the newly swept cement before the Buddha's feet. As I watched each flame popping to life, my thighs throbbed. I stood in the shade at the back of the courtyard and spread my legs wide so as not to aggravate the sores. Shapes of light stencilled by the prayer flags filtered into the courtyard.

When the bells started ringing and everyone bowed their heads, I thought of the easiest prayer I knew.

'*Om mane padme hu.*'

I was filled with the vibration of the humming and the reverberation of the bells. I felt restless. I looked up and a ray of light shimmered through the flags above me. I imagined staying anxious forever, my sores continuing to throb; the light would keep shimmering, no one would tell me what I had done wrong, and one day I would get used to it. Across the sea of bowed heads, I watched Buwa's profile as he prayed. His hair had turned white at the roots and his expression was soft. He had changed so much from the boisterous academic I had known growing up. Standing among the elders, he seemed to belong with them now.

Nearby, I spotted Shabnam standing beside her two little sisters, holding the hand of the youngest, who was starting to fidget. Shabnam turned and held up a finger to shush her, smiling in a way that she never did with me. I wanted to embrace her, and Buwa, but there were too many people between us, and neither had been speaking to me much lately. I wondered how much I had missed. I promised myself that, after the ceremony, I would ask them, I would find out, I wouldn't let them go.

At that moment, the humming of all the people around me in the courtyard seemed to rise in unison. But I wasn't a part of it, and hadn't been for a while. I remembered the way Julie described my photograph and thought what a strange thing it was to say. How could anything not be full of life? Everything was full of it.

The Honourable Man

For Nam Le

The honourable man's greatest duty is to his family. It is not so much a prayer as a reminder. On top of the altar, collecting dust on her marble skin, a small statute of Phật Bà frowns austerely. Next to her are the portraits of my parents. Incense powder sheds as I pull the stick out of its plastic tube. I pick up a lighter, strike it once, twice. No. I need a smoke first. I pull on a coat and head outside.

Exhale. A soft grey plume wafts into the still air, swirling in delicate strands. *Inhale.* Watching it against the concrete and brick of my backyard, I imagine the same streams of smoke winding down passages and darkened chambers in my lungs.

I feel a sting as the cigarette fizzles out at my fingertips.

I smoked before I came here too, when I worked as a rickshaw cyclist in Vietnam, determined to pay my own college fees. I used to watch as my cigarette fumes fused with waves of heat and the steam from hot chicken broth, and was carried into the momentum of the city. There were no traffic lights—I would dodge and weave and the older cyclists would swear at me and spit in my face. I didn't respond; one unspoken word is nine words of peace. It was easy not to mind in the din of Sài Gòn, where the shouting matches of a lovers' feud strained against the fluent rap of street marketers, *Hot-coconut-syrup-on-mung-bean-sweet-soup! Hot-coconut-syrup-on-mung-bean-sweet-soup!* and against a thousand different pitches of bells and the deafening rumble of skewed wooden wheels.

Under the market stalls and in the alleyways crammed between apartment buildings, the smell of fish sauce and overripe fruit seeped out, as though from some open wound beneath. It was a city spilling at the seams with a million different bodies crisscrossing and overlapping, glued together beneath the dense heat that blanketed them.

It wasn't until I stepped into the rented brick unit in a southeast suburb of Melbourne, seventeen years ago, that I started to mind: the tattered carpet and the peeling plaster on the walls, the musty smell in the bathroom, and everything I owned in a fake Nike sportsbag by the door.

Somewhere out of sight, a lawnmower starts up. I crumple the cigarette into the ashtray and fragments of ash continue to smoulder feebly. I have not turned on the ducted heating all winter—a waste of electricity for only one person. The honourable man withstands small nuisances in order to conquer large adversities.

At twelve minutes past five, the doorbell rings. The air freshener I had sprayed earlier hits my nostrils and I feel nauseous. I rub my damp hands on my pants and they drag against the cotton. The doorknob turns with a metallic scrape and my insides grind like a chain of teeth as the door clicks open. 'Son.'

I was fourteen when the soldiers destroyed my province. I woke up to my mother combing her hair, pulling it over her left shoulder and brushing down its length nine times, her lucky number, before twisting it into a bun in one quick, reflexive movement. It calmed me to watch her like this. She had already opened the windows, filling the house with all the places the wind had been. There were valleys in Sơn Mỹ, and swells and rises. It was a two-minute peace. I learned how that world could shatter with the sudden crack of a gunshot and the snap of a spine as it breaks in two, draped over my back. I lay in a ditch for ten hours, sinking into the warmth of the mud, losing feeling in my limbs as they numbed under the weight of my mother's body, counting the thuds of my pulse, too loud, inside my head. I slowly became consumed with envy for the empty bodies around me, oblivious and safe.

To this kind of world I brought a new and innocent life. Every time I look at my son, there is debt.

※

Tuyết often talked about the fight we had when our son was a year old. My cousins from Tây Ninh had written to us again, asking for money. It was a bad time: we had our baby, Tuyết was not working and we had monthly remittances to send to her family. She accused me of being selfish and we fought for so long that I could no longer remember what exactly we were arguing about.

Tuyết went to the door, carrying the baby and her handbag. We were shouting. She threatened divorce. I lunged and pulled the baby out of her arms. She has told me about this scene so many times that I see myself now as an outsider looking in. I held our son around the belly, thrusting him forwards as though to drop him.

'Nothing's wrong with us. We had no problems until he came. What's wrong with us is this child!' I shouted.

The words rang false to me when she repeated them later. Flat and strange words. She said that I was going to throw him. I remember her screaming in such terror that it shocked me out of my anger. I gave the child back to her and fled from the house.

The next day, when I came back, we sat in the backyard on patio chairs. She was quiet and formal. She said that we had to talk. It was her hope, for years, until she finally left, that talking would provide a solution, if the right words were said.

That morning, I told her everything at once, and tried again later in different ways, but they were already dead words. I said that I had hated life for a long time, that I had thought about suicide many times, but had been weighed down by more and more responsibilities that kept me from it. I said it was a mistake to have had a child.

Tuyết stared out at the back fence as I talked, her expression hard and unflinching. She said nothing after I finished. I looked at her face for clues, for a way out of our deadlock, but all I could see was how old we were getting. Her face was wider and more lined. Her lips, more purple than pink, slack in a way I hadn't seen before. I had always pictured her talking, smiling, laughing, frowning, kissing. When I first met her, she had been popular, surrounded by a large family, courted by many suitors and visited by many women for advice.

Neither of us spoke now; we were surrounded by silence for miles, stretching in every direction, for years ahead. A pine branch scraped against the corrugated plastic roofing above us. She had nothing more to say. She never looked pretty and lively to me again.

It is raining heavily outside and my son stands close to the door, his hair flat and his eyes shadowed. He is in school uniform, but the clothes are not his; they are too loose for him, the pants too short. The last time I saw him, two years ago, I had pulled him by the neck and dragged him out this door. He had looked fixedly, unashamedly at me and I had wanted to destroy him.

'Come in,' I say now.

He walks through the door and hesitates before sitting down on the couch by the altar. The leather groans beneath his weight. He opens his mouth to speak, but I am not ready.

171

'I'll be right back,' I say.

My hands are shaking again, but I cannot go outside to smoke. Under the vapid light in the bathroom, my face is wan and papery. I slap water on my cheeks and drops slide down the pockmarked surface, lingering in folds of loosened skin, collecting on my chin, then slipping off one by one onto my shirt. I should change into a cleaner one anyway. I hurry to the wardrobe, already short of breath. I see the old white singlets and polos that I have owned for more than a decade, and cannot remember which ones are stained. Finally, I reached for a blue button-down shirt I have not worn for a long time.

When I return to the living room, my son seems graver than before. He looks like me in so many ways, and carries some of the same terrible burden. For a father's lifetime eating salt, a son's lifetime thirsting water.

I ask after his health and he replies guardedly, his Vietnamese uncertain. A muscle spasms in his jaw.

'I promised Má I would come here,' he says.

I ask, 'What about you?'

'I don't owe you anything.'

In a flash, I have the reflexive urge to yell at him, but it is fainter now, as though worn out from use. I feel us both making the same calculation. My quick anger, his defiance, a shouting match, a slammed door, and then, two years later, my shock again at how his face has changed. I am convinced that we have been moving back, irreparably, to that same place. The words I have been practising all day burn like embers on my tongue as they fall out.

'Come home.'

The words catch in my throat and I feel my eyes stinging with the force of holding them there. He draws back. A neighbour's phone rings, shrill and rhythmic, in the darkness outside.

'No,' he says.

'Come home, and it will be different.' I feel scales hardening on my lips and press my teeth across them.

'I know it's hard.' I look at my son again and realise I no longer know all the words to any prayers. *With every hardship ...* I say to myself, but after that my mind slips back to its vacant screen. 'But if you say yes, it can be done. We can forget what happened. If you say yes, we can find a way.'

His eyes are puddles of black. Nothing moves in his face— his severe brow and concave cheeks. Behind him the window rattles. The rain is full of acid. In the slow descent of evening, streaks of water blur on the windowpanes and the room dims. It occurs to me that I never finished the prayer to Phật Bà, that the stick of incense has yet to dissolve into dusty vapour, to lift and curve in graceful wisps. There are only old ashes on the altar and stumps of incense sticks that I lit some time ago in the ceramic pot. I think about which prayers they had carried, which hopeful pleas, and how those possibilities had drifted away with a word.

Whitewashed

At uni, I was obsessed with a girl in a way that I sometimes thought was sexual. Michaela sat next to me in a writing workshop. She had a delicate, pointy face, and the left side of her head was shaved. On the other side, her hair hung in blonde tendrils.

She wrote weird stories with no endings. There was one about a girl who follows a bartender to Portsea, where the two of them stay holed up in his shitty beach shack for two months, having sex and cooking Chinese food. Another one about a girl who hates her superficial friends and sits alone in an op shop. One day a Vietnam vet asks her for a ciggie.

The first time I talked to Michaela, she invited me to get a coffee with her. The coffee shop was a window in the wall. A big, heavily bearded guy hulked at the window. 'Hey,' he said in a raspy voice.

Michaela ordered two espressos, and told me that the beans were cultivated in the Ethiopian highlands, just west of Jimma, and half-soaked for a day before drying.

'We only use half-soaked beans,' added the guy, making me think of socks.

Michaela told me on the way back to class that she did social media for the café and showed me photos on her phone with captions like *Our lives begin to end the day we become silent about things that matter. – Martin Luther King, Jr.*

'Cool,' I said.

Over the next couple of weeks, Michaela and I always sat next to each other in the workshop and I found myself taking note of what she wore. A chunky grey jumper with thick cuffs, from which her pale, fine hands poked out. A velvet-collared shirt over a thin woollen singlet. I also liked the tone of wonder in her voice, and the way she drawled.

The day we were workshopping her Portsea-bartender story, the professor said something like, 'What we can see in the draft are sketches of two very dynamic characters who have a lot to say, but they need to be imbued with more confidence to really sharpen and propel the central question of the story, which is…' Her hands circled, her wrists twisting as she spoke, as if she was unfurling a large ball of wool.

'I can't make them what they're not,' said Michaela.

She ran her fingers through her half a head of hair.

The first time we went out properly, at night, Michaela commented on the story I had written that was set in Vietnam, about a traditional medicine woman who treated a child struck by lightning.

'Vi, I can really feel your connection to Vietnam,' said Michaela. 'There's a realness, a feeling, that isn't in made-up stories. You know what I mean?'

'Oh yeah.'

'So how do you know her?'

'Who?'

'The medicine woman.'

We were in Brunswick, sitting on iron stools in a bar called Naked for Satan. Michaela wore a black silk top, leather pants and the velvet-collared shirt tied around her waist. I looked to the side and counted the freckles on the back of a guy's hand next to me at the bar.

'I don't know her, but she's a legend in my family's old village.' I turned back to her. 'The ancestral village.'

'Were you born there?'

For some reason I said yes.

'Cool.'

I thought it was sexual because I liked looking at her body, especially the bow of her red lips. As she talked, I stared at the fine blonde hairs on her forehead.

In February, I invited Michaela to go with me to Springvale's Lunar New Year festival. I hadn't been there since I was twelve, but it was fun showing Michaela the dragon dance and the lucky envelope trees, and laughing at the Asian teeny-bopper kids in thinned, dip-dyed hair. Everyone stared at Michaela when she had her palm read, tried five different dishes she didn't really like and lost about twenty dollars in the coin-toss booth.

In the afternoon, Viet musicians went on stage to sing love ballads and traditional songs. Drunk men were watching from Café Baguette, nursing beers and shouting comments over the music: 'It's not like how it used to be!' 'Musicians these days all get plastic surgery!' 'She has lips the size of her arse!' 'They're messed up in the head!'

We watched a woman playing a traditional song on the *dàn tranh,* a Vietnamese zither. Michaela kept nodding her head even though there was no beat.

'That's really cool, really interesting,' she said enthusiastically.

After the final song, the festival organiser stood up to commend us for carrying on the culture of our mothers' blood in a strange country. No one had made us more proud, he said, than the twenty-eight students who scored above ninety in their final school exams. As twenty-eight Viet kids in school blazers filed up on stage to shake his hand, Michaela chuckled into her fingerless gloves.

At dusk, the musicians packed up and the speaker system played Top 40 hits again. The teeny-bopper kids started walking out to Springvale station, carrying large stuffed pandas and Pikachus.

I had to drive Dad home because he had been drinking at the festival. I made him sit in the back because Michaela was in the front, next to me. Mum hadn't come to the festival because she'd had a doctor's appointment for her back— she'd been in pain for as long as I could remember, from her work at a packaging factory. When I dropped Michaela off in Camberwell, Dad stared after her.

'Why does the white girl like you so much?'

'What? We're friends.'

'Why is her hair like a druggie's, huh? Is she a bad girl?'

'Oh my god, it's called style, Dad.'

'What, do people in Camberwell not have enough money to style *all* of their hair?'

He wheezed and the smell of yeast wafted to the front of the car.

'Heaps of young people have hair like hers.'

'Is she one of the gay?'

I huffed, the way Mum did, to make him stop, 'You don't know anything.'

'What don't I know?'

'Oh my god, you're so annoying.'

'You think I don't know anything, huh? You think I don't know why you go to the festival this year for? You think nobody knows you're Asian if you go with a gay druggie?'

'You're drunk.'

'*Do not disrespect your father!*' he screamed, and banged the car door with his fist.

I lost the feeling in my arms. For a moment, I panicked. I

was glad he couldn't see my face from the back seat.

'You think I am stupid, Vi? Why don't you let me speak to your friend? You think I can't speak English? You are corrupted in the head. The druggie kid has corrupted you. Who do you think is on your side? The white people?'

In the rear-vision mirror, I could see the look of concentration on his face as he tried to figure out who had wronged him, his small, dark eyes scanning the surroundings for a victim, his cheekbones bulging from his swollen, angry face.

I suddenly remembered the same look from an incident ten years ago, when I was eleven, sitting in the passenger seat at a drive-through McDonald's. The queue was slow and he was fuming. Suddenly, the car behind moved forward and hit us.

In a flash, Dad leaped out of our car and screamed at the driver whose car had hit us. '*Get out!*'

I watched through the rear-vision mirror as an old man with snowy-white hair and large, brown age spots on his face stumbled out, mumbling incoherently at my dad. Instantly, I felt shame flood my body.

Dad's gaze was focused on the old man. The next moment, he was over at the drive-through window, banging on the plastic shield protecting the cashier, a shellshocked girl who looked about fifteen. Soon the manager came to persuade Dad to wait in the carpark while our food was prepared.

Watching through the window, I tried to convince myself of his childishness. I rehearsed a cool-headed lecture I would give him one day, when he was in a good mood, about what went wrong and how he should have handled the situation. I was used to playing all kinds of tricks on myself so as not to be scared when he was angry. He finally came back to the car.

'These people are so dumb,' he said vehemently, as he snapped on his seatbelt.

'*Mm-hm*,' I replied, my tone as noncommittal as I could manage.

I heard somebody yell 'Fucking chinks' as we left the carpark. At home, the two of us ate our McChicken meals in front of the TV. It was one of the nights when Mum had acupuncture and physiotherapy until late.

'Does it taste strange to you?' he said. He put down the burger. I could tell from his wild eyes that his anger was returning.

'No…no, not at all. It's really good,' I said, and gulped down the rest of my burger. Eventually he resumed eating too.

For the first time, I didn't enjoy the fries, but I ate all of them as quickly as I could and waited until I got to the bathroom to breathe properly again. Many times since then, I've hoped that someone made sure the white-haired old man got home safely.

I glanced at the rear-vision mirror again now. Dad had finally fastened onto the cause of his troubles.

'You're an insolent girl, you always have been. It's impossible to teach you. Nothing will cure you,' he snapped.

The word insolent in Vietnamese, *mất dạy*, is much sharper than the English translation, because it contains notions of disobedience and a lack of filial piety, the worst faults a son or daughter could have. *Mất dạy* also means uneducated, poorly raised. It is like saying that someone is rotten to the core.

When he realised I wasn't going to respond, he slumped in the back seat, muttering to himself. At home, I cried in the bathroom with my knuckles between my teeth, hoping my parents couldn't hear me through the thin walls. In the morning, Dad asked if I wanted to go out for breakfast with him, and I said yes. At the café outside the local mall, he smoked and read the newspaper on his iPad, and I ate scrambled eggs, bacon and a hash brown as quickly as I could, and didn't remind him that I had asthma.

When uni started again in March, my professor set up a meeting for me with a business adviser at a big professional services firm in the city. I saw Michaela before the meeting and confessed that I was nervous.

'About what?'

'The meeting.'

'Do you have to call it a meeting? What is it really?'

'We're getting lunch.'

'So it's just lunch. Who is he again?'

'He works at this big firm I'd like to work at.'

'Oh, that's who he is? Does he even have a name?'

'What's wrong?'

'Nothing. God, you're such a cocksucker.'

She smiled at me; her teeth seemed whiter than usual against the red lipstick.

She was irritated that I wouldn't go to a party with her that night. I had a shift at a dim sum restaurant, and knew I would be too tired afterwards. People always yelled at me from both sides of the floor, and my feet hurt from the beat between the kitchen and the tables.

The next morning, I drove Mum to the Springvale remittance office. She was sending five hundred dollars to our family in Vietnam. Before we left the house, we sat on her bed and spread out the cash, bank statements and receipts.

'Auntie Trang's husband, Đức, do you remember him? His right hand got caught in a factory machine last week and he has to get surgery,' she said.

She put on her glasses and picked up the spiral-bound notebook where she kept a record of all her expenses.

'They're going to sew skin from his bottom onto his fingers. I know, it's disgusting. He won't be able to work for a while.'

She pinched her forehead and reached for a bottle of tablets by the bed.

'We have to buy more fish-oil tablets for your grandparents too. Their joints are hurting lately. Can you get them?'

'Okay, but you know you can get them yourself. It's really easy, you just have to say fish oil.'

'They won't understand me,' she said dismissively.

'Yes, they will. I've heard you say it, *fish oil*, you say it fine.'

'Just go, okay, Vi?'

She checked another page in the spiral notebook.

'I'm not going to collect the lottery until April,' she said. She was part of *hụi*, lottery game, in which a group of Vietnamese, usually friends or family, pools its money and each person takes a turn to collect the lottery when they most need it.

'How much did our groceries cost last week?' she continued, as if to herself.

'I don't know.'

'I shouldn't have bought those new orthopaedic shoes. Do you know if your dad has any money left?'

I wanted to beg her to stop talking about money.

'No, I don't. Why don't you ask him?' I said testily.

She looked at me, her lips pursed.

'What?' I glared at her.

After the remittance office, I left her in the Chemist Warehouse carpark. When I got back in the car with the jumbo tub of fish-oil tablets, she was still muttering numbers under her breath, the spiral notebook held up to her face, the other hand massaging her temples. She would soon make a mistake and ask me to look over the numbers. I tried to swallow my frustration. To distract myself, I stuck my hand inside the tub of little capsules and rolled my fingers around. The capsules rattled gently, plastic against plastic. How many were in there? Say, eighty, a hundred, more, too many to count. Mum smacked my hand and told me to start the car.

'So do you spend all your time sucking dicks?'

I jumped. Michaela was peering at the screen over my shoulder. I had gone to the library to edit an application for an internship. I glanced at the guy studying on the other side of the table, and laughed loudly.

Michaela sat down next to me and twisted my laptop towards her.

'*What has especially attracted me to PwC is not only its number-one ranking as a worldwide business consulting provider…*' Michaela read. '*Da da da.*'

'Hey.'

'*The qualities I have to offer this firm include…*' Michaela held up a fist by her mouth and wanked an imaginary penis. I looked up at the guy again.

'All right, all right.'

'Hey, I never knew about your strength in advisory services.'

'Yeah, okay.'

She held the imaginary penis again and licked up its shaft.

'Let's go,' I said. 'I'm gonna be late for work if we want to have coffee first.'

I packed up my things and we headed out into the courtyard.

'Speaking of cocksucking, that reminds me.' She paused dramatically.

'What?' I stared at her as we walked.

'I ran into *Colby* yesterday,' she said, rolling her eyes. Colby, her ex.

'Oh yeah?'

'Yeah, he asked for a lift home.'

'Okay.'

'Then he made me stop at Woolies, and I didn't even need to get anything. I was being fucking *nice.*'

'He thinks the world revolves around him,' I said

automatically. I had said this before about her exes.

'You know what he wanted to buy?'

'No, what?'

'Condoms. He bought fucking *condoms*. He made me drive him to Woolies to buy him *condoms*.'

'What a little shit.'

'You know what else he said?' Her voice was heavy with sarcasm.

'What?'

'He said you're hot for an Asian.'

She turned to watch me intently. I felt instantly scared and pleased at the same time, and was a beat too late in my response:

'He's trying to make you jealous.'

'Yeah, he really needs to get over it,' she grunted.

'He's obsessed with you,' I said, relieved.

When she stopped talking, I allowed myself to relish the thrill that Colby had called me hot. For an Asian.

As we walked across one of the Melbourne University lawns, I spotted a sea of bright blue T-shirts, where the kids from the Association of Southeast Asian Nations were sitting, the Asian culture club. The last time ASEAN had a barbeque on the lawn, one of the girls was going to give me the spiel, but my friend Kieu intervened, saying, 'Don't bother, Vi's completely whitewashed.' She smiled at me and the other girl laughed. It was a compliment. Then I pretended that I was in a hurry to get to the tram stop.

Kieu always made me feel guilty. I knew Kieu from my

first high school, in Springvale, a hub for the Vietnamese and Chinese communities. She was the one who started calling me Vi in Year Seven, even though I had an English name, and it stuck. Kieu was my best friend for a year. She didn't seem to care what anyone thought of her. She wore pants that fitted badly, when all the girls at school, including me, were folding our skirts up around the waist so they'd be shorter. While I dreaded being weighed in PE class, Kieu's mum was making her drink malt to gain weight. She used to crawl underneath tables and prank us by jiggling the fat on our calves. She had really bad acne then, and a weird mullet haircut, which she straightened every morning. We pranked each other and argued all the time. Even though we each had our separate groups, nothing was more fun than fake-fighting with each other.

In eighth grade, some of the boys thought they were going to join gangs. Kieu's two older brothers were in one. When Kieu tried to convince me that she had joined the Springy Boys, I tried as best I could to deflate her ego.

'What kind of gang is it? Do you guys get together for coffee? Sleepovers?'

'It's not about what we do. It's like how we protect each other.'

'What do you need protection from?'

'The other gangs.'

'What other gangs?'

'I don't know,' said Kieu. 'I mean, if you ever got in trouble, I would protect you.'

'Oh yeah?'

'Yeah. You're one of us. I mean, you know me. So the gang would protect you, because you're my sis. No questions asked.'

'Well, thanks for that.'

My happiest memories of high school were the evenings after school when we walked together to the bus stop, bickering and annoying each other. I confused myself once by thinking that I might be in love with her. Right before I left, I wanted to tell her.

We'd become a little sweeter then, because I was leaving. On the last day of term, school finished at lunchtime and we hung out on the outdoor basketball court. I sat cross-legged and Kieu lay down with her head on my lap. I tried to absentmindedly touch her hair, the greasy, mullet-cut hair that I so often made fun of. The rough concrete irritated my thighs—I was wearing a skirt—but I didn't want to move; I didn't want her to sit up.

As Michaela and I continued across the lawn, I pretended I didn't see Kieu among the ASEAN kids. We swept by, and I knew we looked good, with our racial contrast, her half-shaved head, our lipstick, and our skirts that were short in the front and long in the back, lifting and swooping over the lawn.

After coffee, I took the train back to Springvale for my evening shift at Gold Leaf Restaurant. Colby sent me a Facebook friend-request as I was waiting at the platform at Melbourne Central. I knew Michaela would see it if I accepted his friend-request, especially on the same day she'd told me he said I was hot. For an Asian. In fact, I could imagine her taunting him to do it: *If you think she's hot, why don't you add her?* I put my phone in my bag.

The Cranbourne train arrived and I got on. It was full, so I leaned against a railing by the door.

More passengers got on at South Yarra and Caulfield stations. By the time we were at Oakleigh, I was pushed near a middle-aged woman who was yelling on her phone.

'Yeah, I'm just about to get off. Third carriage, third carriage, or maybe fifth, I don't know. I said *fifth*!' she shouted.

She was wearing an orange parka and a Pandora bracelet on the wrist holding the phone. Her short blonde hair was soft and frizzy.

'Oh my god, *fifth*. I can't hear with all these kids around, these fucking rude kids,' she continued.

A woman wearing a suit and glasses, standing next to her, spoke up.

'Hey, that's my son.'

'What a polite boy, what a *polite* boy. He sees all these people standing up and he can't get out of his seat. Real polite boy you've got there.'

'*Don't* touch my son.'

A guy in his late twenties, cropped blond hair and a broad face, standing beside me, chimed in.

'There are gonna be plenty of seats when we get to the next station, okay? Then you can get a seat,' he said. There was a tremor in his voice.

'I'm getting off at Hughesdale,' the woman said quickly,

mercifully no longer shouting. The next stop. She glanced at him, then at me, and broke into a grin.

'Ha! Look, he's too lazy to jerk off, he's only got a gook! Can't even get a regular girlfriend!' She laughed, looking around to see who would join her. I heard several groans.

'So sad, he's gotta get a gook! Ha!'

I felt all the eyes in the carriage turn to me. A woman sitting nearby glanced at me and looked away when our eyes met.

'What are you talking about?' I snapped. 'What—'

'*Wha yo tah king*,' she said, delightedly. '*Wah yooo, wah chao ba yo, do do do do*.'

She stretched her eyes wide at the corners with her fingers as she jabbered.

'Honestly, shut the hell up,' said the guy next to me.

'*Wah chao, wah nice boy, wah nice boy*,' she mocked. 'Ha! Go back China *ho ho ho*. We go back China.'

'Don't—' I began, but I had no words.

'Why don't you go back to Hong Kong? Why did you come to this country? This is our country,' she said.

'Fuck off!' said the guy next to me.

'Can't you get an Aussie girlfriend? You had to get a gook, you poor pathetic man,' she said. 'How small is it that you can't even get a regular girlfriend? You sad man.'

He started laughing, affecting an incredulous tone.

'You're fucking scum!' someone yelled from the end of the carriage.

When I saw Hughesdale platform through the windows, I let out a sigh.

The woman stopped laughing as the train stopped.

I pressed myself against the railing as she shoved past, elbowing the guy next to me on the way out. As the door closed and the train started up, he caught my eye.

'Are you okay?' he asked, frowning.

'Yeah,' I said shrilly. Then I realised the rest of the carriage, all silent, were expecting a more satisfying answer. 'Can't let people like that get you down.'

He smiled. 'That's right, that's right. Let's put it behind us.'

I got off at the next stop, even though it wasn't mine. I sat on a bench on the platform, where no one had witnessed what had just happened. It struck me that I would have missed that train if I had stopped at the ASEAN stand to say hello to Kieu. I unlocked my phone and thought of calling her, even though it wasn't really an option. She wouldn't understand why I had called. *What's wrong with you?* I could hear her say. I hadn't called her since I'd left Springvale High and gone to an all-girls private school. I'd called her from the bathroom during my first week at the new school.

'Hey, do you miss me yet?' I asked.

'Are you in a *bathroom*?' she said incredulously.

'What? No.'

'Yeah you are, I can tell, it's all echoey.'

'Well, I don't know why. I'm not.'

'What's wrong with you? Don't you have any friends?' She started laughing.

We had always pretended to be mean to each other, but I couldn't take it then.

We talked less and less after that, and then, many months later, we agreed to meet for lunch. It was strange because it was so formal and deliberate; it wasn't like walking to the same bus stop or leaving food in each other's lockers over the weekend so it'd go bad. I didn't feel like I could say she was ugly or anything like that. She had never been serious with me before. In fact, she was perhaps the only person who didn't take me seriously. After the lunch, Kieu insisted on paying, and I didn't know why, but it felt cold.

Instead, I messaged Michaela:

woow Colby just added me

he's trying so hard to get your attention

I saw speech bubbles as she typed and felt heartened that she was answering me straightaway.

What a loser she messaged back.

Then I accepted Colby's friend-request and boarded the next train.

A few days later, Michaela had a fight with her mum. She was crying on the phone to me and asked if she could crash at my place. When I picked her up in Camberwell, she was sitting on the front step of her house, her hair mussed and her eyes leaking eyeliner. Her tattered clothes and old boots looked out of place against the neat, landscaped front garden.

'She's such an anal bitch,' Michaela said in the car.

'What happened?'

'I'm fucking twenty-one years old and I still have to tell my mum where I'm going and when I'll be home, and she goes ape-shit whenever I'm late.'

'Well…'

'You have no idea how controlling she is. She has no idea who I am, only what she wants me to be.'

'Mm–hm.'

'What?'

'I'm not going to say anything bad about your mum.'

'Oh my God.' She put her legs up on the dashboard and closed her eyes.

She brightened up once we arrived at my house. It was the first time she'd been there. I felt uncomfortable when she opened the flyscreen with the Chinese character for luck strung through the mesh. The smell of mum's cooking hit me, fishier than I remembered. I was suddenly anxious she had made *bún mắm*, shrimp noodle soup, and left it to simmer on the stove while she went for acupuncture.

I led Michaela to the kitchen, the largest open space in the house and eyed the pear-patterned tarpaulin on our table, the almanac of girls modelling the traditional *áo dài*, and the altar in the corner with three portraits of our ancestors and a statuette of the deity *phật bà*.

Michaela ran her hand through her hair and leaned back in her seat.

'Your place is really, really cool. It's so real.'

She got up and studied the altar, stroking the fake jade of the *phật bà*.

'Don't.'

'What?'

'Don't touch that.' I took a breath, then exhaled loudly.

'Come on, you can put your stuff in my room.'

Michaela insisted on waiting for Mum to come home to have the shrimp noodle soup together, but by then Mum was too tired to eat. I didn't know what good the acupuncture was doing, if it meant she got home late and dazed every night. She barely registered Michaela's presence at first.

'What's the matter? Let her eat. Serve her,' Mum said to me in Vietnamese. I had followed Mum to her bedroom, where she was methodically taking off her uniform: thick, bright safety clothing. I winced when I saw the red bruises on her back from her cupping therapy.

'But she wants to eat *with* you, she's been waiting for you,' I said.

'What for?'

'I don't know, to get to know you.'

She held out a strip of white medical tape. 'Here, put the Salonpas on my back. What am I going to say to her?'

'Anything, it doesn't matter.'

Mum came back out to the kitchen with me, in an old fleece tracksuit, and served the soup for me and Michaela. She filled a mug with hot water for herself and sat down.

'Have you had before?' Mum asked Michaela, pointing at the soup.

'No, but it smells delicious!'

She sipped from her spoon uncertainly. It was an especially pungent soup, which even I found too strong.

'How was acupuncture, Mrs Ho?' Michaela asked. 'I'm really interested, I'm thinking about trying it myself.'

'You want acupuncture?' Mum asked.

'Yes.'

'Why?'

'It's supposed to be really good for relaxation, skin health, maybe even weight loss,' Michaela said.

Mum looked at me, confused; Michaela had spoken too quickly. I translated it back to her.

'Oh, I don't know that,' Mum said to Michaela.

'She gets it for her back pain,' I explained.

'My knee too, from work. I stand all day. My fingers stiff,' Mum said, massaging her knuckles. 'I ask Vi to goggle doctor for me. He said I need three times a week.'

'Goggle doctor? What's a—'

'She meant Google,' I explained.

'Oh, Google!' Michaela burst out laughing. 'I was trying to imagine what a goggle-doctor was! Some sort of new Eastern medicine.'

'*Nó cười Mẹ hả?*' Mum asked me. *Is she laughing at me?*

'No, she thinks you said something else,' I said, as Michaela kept giggling.

Mum excused herself; nine was her usual bedtime anyway. She had to get up at five in the morning. I poured the rest of the soup into plastic containers and threw out most of Michaela's bowl. She had barely touched it.

We stayed at the kitchen table doing some uni work. Dad came back around eleven-thirty, smelling of cigarettes, his face red. He headed straight for the fridge to grab a box of leftover fried noodles, ignoring us.

195

'Hi, Mr Ho,' Michaela said.

He turned, glared at her and left the room.

'He's been drinking. Don't worry about it,' I said. She raised her eyebrows, amused.

When I went to brush my teeth, things about the bathroom that I hadn't noticed before bothered me: the bathtub was cracked, with yellow stains. The shower curtain was slick in places; I couldn't recall if we'd ever washed it. There was some sort of dark gunk in the corners of the bathroom tiles.

Michaela's floral Ted Baker toiletry bag stood out against the brown and beige of our bathroom. I made sure the door was closed and nudged the bag open—she had left it unzipped. I noticed an expensive bottle of moisturiser and considered using it, but then realised she might recognise the smell on my skin.

That night, as I lay in bed, Michaela on a mattress on the floor beside me, she started speaking into the dark.

'I think I'd like growing up poor.'

What could I respond? *Why would you?* Or, *Why are you bringing that up in my house?* I stayed silent.

'You could really get to know the basics of life,' said Michaela. 'Basic happiness.'

'What does that mean?'

'It's like, when you don't have money, and you don't have the trappings of wealth, the superficiality, the materialism, you're really free. I find that poor people have so much more love and loyalty.'

She leaned up on my bed, crushing my right arm.

'You know, you've got to let go of chasing conventional success. Why don't you define success for yourself?'

I looked at her, hovering over my bed, her hair brushing my bare shoulder. I couldn't believe that we were friends, that she needed me when she had family problems, that she wanted to sleep at my house. Although I had been hanging out with her for a long time, her face was still new to me. In the shadows, her blonde hair floated like half a halo next to her face. She was so beautiful. It seemed incredible to be so close to her, and yet I couldn't tell, even then, what exactly it was that she wanted.

My arm had gone numb. When I moved it out from under her, I felt a sudden surge of energy and realised what I had to say to her: that growing up poor has nothing to do with freedom, that I grew up in the back of a milk bar, that Mum put up dividers in the living room, where we slept, and rented out the rest of the rooms to three individual tenants, that she cried when I wanted to go to Grade Six camp, that Dad smashed everything in the kitchen when she reminded him to go to Centrelink. That when I went with Mum to Target to buy new sets of plates the next day, she started crying and then went to wait in the car while I picked out white plates with an orange daisy pattern, that we were surrounded all the time by things that needed to be fixed, that waiting for things to be fixed made us tired and sour, that I had to work hard and do the right thing, bend and mould myself into scholarship applications, act interesting yet obedient, ethnic but assimilated, and that if I was too quiet, didn't speak up, didn't fight back, it was because I was trying to rise up, and had to get beaten down first.

If I didn't feel jealous of Michaela, it was because I never thought that I could be her equal. But I didn't say anything, I wasn't ready yet, and before I knew it, the beautiful bow lips came bearing down on me.

Hot Days

During the summer, Linh squatted in the kitchen of Hòa Trân Café and pressed her bare back to the stone sink. Customers stopped coming in and even the ice melted in the tubs of sweet drinks in the fridge. By the end of the day, the cubes of grass jelly had shrivelled, layers of wrinkled film on their sides, and Linh had to throw it all into the bushes behind the café.

The vegetation was dying. Something new and thick was growing from the glucose and gelatine dumped into the bushes. In the open courtyard, where Linh had to wipe down the sweating tables, she could think of nothing but old skin and she wanted to cry from the heat.

The sun favoured Ngày Mới province that year and it was bad for business. Families slept on the floor with the fans on. Boys went to drink beer under trees by the river bank and woke up weeping from hangovers and peeling skin. The Văns' youngest son fell down an old war tunnel and was only discovered hours later, hot and dead.

One afternoon, her boss, Bác Phong, found Linh by the sink and offered to give her the rest of the day off.

'No, please don't make me go home,' said Linh.

'Don't worry, you'll still get your pay.'

'Please, no. My mother will kill me. Let me stay. I'll clean the tables again.'

'Your mother will have a problem with it?'

'I'll get in trouble for being lazy. Please…'

Linh stood up into the sun and felt it sear her face.

'How about I close up for the day?' said Bác Phong. 'What will Nga say to that?'

'Can I please use the sink to wash my face before I go?'

'Of course.'

Linh bent over the sink and lowered her hands to cup the water left over from when she had washed bean sprouts earlier.

'Heavens, you can use the tap.'

He turned on the tap and Linh craned her neck to catch the water. Bác Phong looked away as she stuck out her tongue to lap at it.

When Linh first came to apply for a job at Hòa Trân Café three years ago, she was wearing her mother's blouse, the button-down one Nga saved for special occasions. It had pointed, conical structures for breasts. Linh couldn't fill it out like Nga did; even though they had similar small bodies, Linh's was flatter and more angular.

'You are Nga's daughter?' Bác Phong had asked the girl in the oddly fitting blouse.

When he touched the rim of his glasses, Linh had followed the glint of light that leapt across his face into the tree canopy. He spoke slowly and emphatically, without the slack-lipped Ngày Mới accent. His stance was the same, shoulders even and arms out front, as though he were waiting to catch something. Linh replied, 'Yes, that's me.' She was taken aback by how loud her voice sounded. She always thought of herself as quiet, not much to say in class and awkward with the other girls, so they never really listened to her. Not that the girls were cruel, but Linh demanded so little attention that they did not focus, looking past her, as if she were heat haze on the highway.

'I can cook,' she continued tentatively. 'I can clean. I help my mother at home.'

Linh soon knew that she would be a waitress her whole life. Her forearms were wide and strong, just right for carrying trays. The yellow-and-white-striped dish cloth moved smoothly about her body: tucked under her armpit, slung over her shoulder, balled up in her fist, or pressed between her chin and her chest.

When Linh came home, Nga was still sitting at the sewing machine. She swung an arm back and jabbed Linh in the stomach.

'What are you doing home early? What did you do to disgrace me?'

'Bác Phong closed the café because there were no customers.'

'So you're going to sit around like an idiot?'

'No.'

'Then go and cut the grass.'

Behind the taro field, they grew grass for the cows. Linh bent over to grasp a fistful of tall grass, then hooked her scythe around the roots. The grass blades, almost as thick as coconut branches, crunched and split into fine hairs. Linh had forgotten to wear gloves and soon her hands were soaked in sap. She sang a made-up tune as she worked: *disgrace-me, disgrace-me, disgrace-me*, she chanted. *Disgrace-me, disgrace-me, disgrace…* Linh slumped into the grass as the familiar rhythm rocked her to sleep. She could not tell how much time had passed when she faded back in, gaping at the sun, and began scything again.

The next day, Bác Phong announced that they would hold live music nights in the café. A keyboardist and a traditional singer arrived that evening. The singer, a woman, wore a tight *áo dài* dress and white powder on her face.

'Please welcome our musicians.'

Bác Phong introduced them as old friends from his childhood in Sài Gòn before the war ended in 1975. With the heat of the night, the powder on the singer's right cheek clumped and slid down to her chin, where it formed a crust. Twenty customers came and went.

Afterwards, Linh stayed back to sweep up the peanut shells, rice-paper spice packets and cigarette butts strewn across the courtyard. Bác Phong was strumming his guitar in the corner. When she finished sweeping, Linh stood in front of him, staring.

'Ever seen a guitar before?' Bác Phong said, picking a chord.

'No.'

'Beautiful, isn't it?'

'Yes.'

She had heard plenty of music before, but always from a machine. She never imagined the instruments that wrung sounds out of the air.

'Do you want to learn?'

'What?'

'Do you want to learn how to play the guitar?'

'Me?'

Bác Phong pursed his lips, 'Yes. Why don't you come to my house for a lesson on Saturday morning? Would Nga be okay with that?'

Linh did not know how to reply.

'I'll tell you what. Let me handle this. I'll visit Nga tomorrow and ask her myself,' Bác Phong offered.

Linh supposed that he went to their house during the day, while she was working at the café. When she came home that evening, she almost expected the house to look different, to bear a trace of their guest. But nothing was out of place.

Nga was sitting at her sewing table, positioned at its usual six o'clock spot.

'You will wake up two hours early tomorrow to do your chores, then you will catch the eight o'clock bus,' Nga said, her eyes still on fabric in front of her. 'I am going to tell you what to say to the driver and how to get to the house from the bus stop. Listen carefully.'

His home was in Sài Gòn, a forty-five-minute bus ride from Ngày Mới. Linh sat on the bus the next day, jiggling the sticky rice ball that Nga had packed for her breakfast. The windows were closed to stop the dust from getting in. The rice swelled in the heat and she had to lap it out of her sweaty palm. After the last mouthful, she snapped her sticky fingers together. She thought she would die from the heat.

Linh got off at a stop just past Củ Chi. She walked the rest of the way, following the instructions Nga had made her repeat back three times. From down the road, she saw Bác Phong sitting in his front yard under an old orange tree with a dense green canopy. A birdcage hung behind his head. Linh had never seen a kept bird before. Its feathers were green with a splash of red on the neck.

'Welcome, Linh. Sit down,' Bác Phong said. He already had the guitar cradled in his lap.

Linh stepped into the shade of the orange tree and shivered. She thought it must be the coolest spot in all of Vietnam. She couldn't smell sugar anymore, only the faint bitterness of orange skin.

'Watch my left hand,' he said.

Linh gazed at his grip on the neck of the guitar. His fingers stretched across the fret and pressed down, white from the pressure. He strummed a chord.

Bác Phong then reached over and placed the guitar in her hands. Linh plucked a string. A note rang out and floated up on a quiver of air. Linh picked the note again, amazed that she could flick the strings and make the heat ripple. She plucked again. Her world seemed marvellous for a moment, as she touched and the thing sang back. *So, so, so, so, so.* Flick and ripple. She forgot her own skin, and the heat, and listened to the note *so*, which seemed to have no beginning or end. Her little brown finger, crooked into the belly of the sound hole, picked until it cramped.

About an hour later, someone called out to Bác Phong from inside the house. Linh raised her head from the guitar and stared at the dark hallway beyond the open door. A woman emerged, in a white pyjama suit with ruffles at the shoulders, as if called forth by the note from the guitar. She had a small face and her hair was tied on one side. She repeated the words, but they were still indistinct.

'No. Medicine is not till one o'clock,' Bác Phong replied.

The woman spoke again. This time, because the phrase was familiar, Linh could make it out: 'What are you doing?' she whined.

'Nothing, I'll be in soon,' said Bác Phong.

The woman took a step back and disappeared into the darkness of the hallway.

'Starting an instrument is always difficult,' Bác Phong said to Linh, picking up the guitar from her lap. He took a deep breath. 'Why don't you come back for another lesson next Saturday?'

Over the following weeks, Linh found her mind slipping back to Bác Phong's fingers, and the vibration of the guitar when she held it, like a live, humming animal in her arms. Her mind dwelt only on the music lessons, and she wondered if it was possible that she had never had any other thoughts at all before. She wiped tables, washed dishes, peeled fruit and candied coconut, thinking all the time of Bác Phong's fingers.

And his glasses too. Nobody wore glasses in Ngày Mới; people just squinted if necessary. Was it the glasses that made Bác Phong's gaze different, or had she never noticed anyone else's eyes before? She imagined fingers inside her head, trying to catch a slimy, wriggling fish that kept leaping into the water. The little wet thing rolled against the nerves in her skull and nestled into her cheek, just in reach of her tongue.

She did not tell anyone about the fish in her head, but one day at the café she asked Trang about Bác Phong's wife.

'She's not from here. I think she's from Sài Gòn. Why?'

Linh told her about the guitar lessons.

'Why is he giving you guitar lessons?'

'I don't know.'

'Don't be so dumb. Why is he giving you guitar lessons?'

Linh was afraid of getting it wrong again. Trang rolled her eyes. She was pouring sugar into pickled lime juice, her long nails flat against the stirring spoon. This week they were painted yellow-green like raw mango.

'I don't think he's giving anyone else guitar lessons. How are you paying him?'

'I'm not paying him.'

'But why is he doing it? It's not like…' Trang clucked and turned around. 'Are you, what, are you touching him?'

'No!'

'You know you probably have to.'

'I can't do that.'

'You don't know how to, do you?' Trang chortled. 'Of course you don't.'

'What do you mean, touching him?'

'Linh. I'm not going to tell you what to do.' Trang fiddled with a piece of old lime, spreading its flesh against the side of the tub. 'I mean, I'll tell you how to start. He'll know what to do then.'

That night, when Linh squatted in the backyard to bathe, she trickled the water slowly down her body. A joint bulged on the side of her right knee and she massaged it, hooking a knuckle underneath the knee, where it was softer, like bands of plastic. She ground her knuckle up and down. If she could just do this every day, Linh thought, her legs might become soft and smooth. The muscles crunched as she rolled them back and forth. She imagined that every touch was colouring her in, giving her texture.

The next Saturday, when Linh arrived, Bác Phong was already sitting in the yard and the front door was open once again. This time Linh felt cold under the orange branches, imagining Bác Phong's wife lurking out of sight, two steps beyond the door, listening. Had he ever taught his wife to play guitar?

She fiddled with the same string while he talked. She strummed as though scratching a scab, itching to be touched. But she still couldn't play chords, couldn't even hold down the strings with her left hand.

Bác Phong reached over and pressed his fingers on top of hers.

She glanced at him and words popped into her head, *I feel very close to you*. She looked at the open door. There hadn't been any sound from the house. Linh leaned forward, but as she did, Bác Phong leaned back and reached for a glass of black coffee perched on the potted plant behind him.

'What does Nga think of the lessons?' he asked.

'She says you are kind.'

'You know, Nga really loves music.'

Linh watched heat waves and string vibrations materialise in the air between her and Bác Phong. She sniffed loudly, arching back so they wouldn't touch her. Beyond them, she spotted the glint of Bác Phong's glasses.

'...in seventy-five when I came to Ngày Mới for the first time. The Communists were looking for families with large estates, so we sold everything in Sài Gòn and came here. I went to the Văn Thủy sugarcane stand every day to see her.'

He was staring at her now.

'You must already know this. Nga must have told you,' he said.

His voice was suddenly softer and he leaned forward, his elbows on his knees, massaging his knuckles anxiously.

'What has she told you?' he implored.

Stunned, Linh didn't say anything. But Bác Phong began to nod slowly, as though gathering some meaning from her expression. He sprang back in his chair and rubbed his thighs, his black slacks riding up.

'It wasn't just me,' he pressed on. 'Nga felt something too. We went on walks together. I came to visit your grandfather's house once and brought eggs for the whole family. Did she tell you about that? Eggs were expensive after seventy-five. But she wouldn't marry me.'

A square of light reflected off his glasses. His eyes were now fixed elsewhere.

All the strands that Linh had strung fell limp, soft like cobwebs, and now she too sat staring off into the canopy of orange. *Wouldn't marry me, marry-me, marry-me.* The words echoed in her head.

'Nga wanted to leave Vietnam, but I still had my family estate to look after. This estate. My brothers have gone. Now it's just me. When Nga married Anh Xuân, his family was going to go to America,' he said.

He turned to Linh.

'You never knew your father. You look a little like him. Has anybody told you? You have his mouth,' he said.

His gaze fell to her lips, and Linh burned with the

realisation of her hideousness. *Look away, look away, look AWAY.* His brow wrinkled and Linh thought he might have heard the shouting in her head, but then he turned away to stare at the road outside his front yard.

'Nobody thought Nga would be with a man like him,' he continued. 'Your father was not a bad man. But he was quiet and secretive. He was never a man of words. Nga couldn't talk to him, not the way she could talk to me.'

Linh had never known her mother to be talkative. She was horrified to see tears in Bác Phong's eyes.

'It was what we did. I spent hours at her sugarcane stand every day, and we talked and talked. She wouldn't let me feed the machine, in case I made a mistake and wasted the sugarcane. There wasn't much to go around in those years. She barely had any food and, although my family had more than most, I didn't eat much that summer at all. I lost a lot of weight. I was chubby back in Sài Gòn, but when I was with Nga all day, we just chewed on sugarcane pulp, and coffee beans, and rice paper, and talked...I began to know her so well I could tell what she was thinking just by looking at her. Can you imagine knowing a person that well? I never did again, not like that.'

He was still staring into the distance and Linh didn't know what to do to remind him she was there. *What-we-did, what-we-did, what-we-did,* she echoed.

'But her choice was simple: she wanted to leave Vietnam. She had you while he went off on a boat for America. He was going to petition for both of you after he had arrived, found a place to live, set up a life. Of course, she never heard from him again. Maybe he died at sea, but more likely he left her.

'I've been coming into Ngày Mới for decades now, and she's been waiting for your father all that time. Wouldn't even look at me again after she married that man. Such an honourable woman. Just the woman to love…

'Are you interested in what I am saying?'

When Linh stood up and walked away, she knew that she could never come back to the orange shade. Her heart filled with shame. She stepped out of the front yard and down the length of the house, forty-two steps. Around the corner, she faced the sun head-on and everything before her swam in the white light. If she stopped counting, she could skip a beat and slip away. Or the heat could dissolve her if she didn't know when to stop. There was so much road, so much time, and such a dry little body. Linh squinted and walked down the other side of the house, *forty-eight, forty-nine, woman-to-love, woman-to-love, one-hundred-and-two, woman-to-love, one-hundred-and-three*, walking in tight, straight steps.

All the way back to the highway, on the bus, and down the dirt road, to the other side of the irrigation ditch to her house, she counted. Linh held her breath as she reached the door and knew Nga would be sitting at the sewing machine on the other side, her arms tense, the lines of muscle running down to her forearm. Every three seconds a knot unravelled, a thrumming sound escaped from her mouth, *th*, and the string, which ran from her lips to a front yard on the edge of town, was plucked and the air shivered.

Nga laid down the pieces of cloth in a neat stack. Finished, she dragged the worktable backwards to catch the moving sliver of light. She sat down and surveyed her new position in the room. A spider's web reflected light in the corner of the room, above the altar. Nga stepped over, climbing a shoe rack on her third step, and waved a duster at the corner. Stretched out, she saw herself covering the length of her wall. Her left foot curled and she held her breath, feeling that she had caught the four walls of her life in the sole of her foot.

When the girl came home and asked about Bác Phong, Nga laughed softly, *th*. Did he tell you about the eggs, she asked, is he still proud of that? You are so dumb, *th*, when are you going to learn? Only believe half of what men tell you, *th*. Now, go and light your father a stick of incense and put on the fan, will you, we're going to die in this heat. *Th.* She gripped the sewing table as though it needed steadying and went back to work.

A Scholar's Hands

Bình stopped the Commodore behind the petrol station, where he wouldn't need a parking ticket. He was a few minutes late, but there was no sign of Tuấn. A white middle-aged woman with ragged hair and pink pants eyed him uneasily through the window as she walked by carrying her Safeway bags. Bình rolled down the window, but there was no breeze on such a humid summer day. He lit a cigarette and pulled out his battered paperback edition of *To Kill a Mockingbird*, the title printed in large white letters on a black background. After a few moments, he let the book drop out of his hand without having registered a word.

He had read the book countless times; holding it now was just a matter of ritual. It had been in the box of Salvos donations he received when he moved into his rented unit five years ago, in 1989. The pages were yellowed but the spine was tight, so he knew it hadn't been read. At first Bình used it as literacy material, flicking through to see which words he could recognise. When a volunteer at the learning centre approved of his copy, he tugged it away from her grasp and shrugged, but he began to try harder to read the book. Slowly, he got a vague idea of the storyline. The idioms became clearer by the fourth or fifth reading. He read it for the eighth time when he was enrolled at university, in the government-sponsored program. By the eleventh reading he was thinking about metaphors.

The passenger door creaked open and the Commodore shook as Tuấn swung his gangling frame inside.

'Fuck you, Tuấn, what took so long?'

'Sorry, sorry. A fiftieth birthday party stayed late.'

Bình spat onto the footpath before rolling up the window.

'Did you at least get paid overtime?'

'Nah,' Tuấn said through gum, 'it wasn't very long.'

'You idiot. Do you think you're doing those people a favour?' Bình reversed the Commodore. 'Cleaning up after their shit ... If you're not getting paid, you're letting them take advantage of you. They think they're so much better than us, but they're only Chinese.'

'They're not so bad.'

'I've seen how you are with them. You have this dumb smile for them, and you say *please* and *thank you* and *sorry* all the time.' Bình switched into an exaggerated Vietnamese accent. 'And they don't do shit for you.'

He glanced at Tuấn, who was picking dirt out from under his fingernails.

'You don't even care!' Bình shouted. He knew he was over-reacting but couldn't help it. He slammed the dashboard with the heel of his palm.

As they headed along the Monash Freeway, neither of them spoke. Around the Chadstone exit, he pushed down on the accelerator to provoke Tuấn, who always drove carefully, below the speed limit.

'Look, man,' Tuấn said heavily, 'I didn't make you drop out.'

Bình turned to look at Tuấn again. Although they were both twenty-eight, Tuấn seemed thinner and more worn, as if he carried every grievance on his loose skin. He was the kid who had fed Bình water when they were strangers on Bidong Island. Bình had woken up from a hellish fever to see Tuấn baring his yellow teeth through the ugliest smile he had ever seen. They were both the first in their family to escape Vietnam and had no one to follow, so when asked where he wanted to settle, Tuấn pinched the skin on his ribs, and said, 'I hear they eat a lot of butter in Australia. I can really fatten up with some butter, hey?' And Bình had followed.

Bình had long fingers and smooth, pale skin. Before he died in the war, Bình's father used to examine his hands, turning them over and tugging at the joints. 'These are your mother's hands. She washed clothes and gutted chicken with her bare hands all day—no matter, they would stay just like this, smooth and white. A scholar's hand,' he once said, then slipped a pen into Bình's palm. 'One scholar is a blessing for his whole village.'

Bình's knuckles were turning white on the steering wheel. 'What the fuck, what does that have to do with anything?'

'You hate working at Cô Năm's grocery shop, Bình. Stop being so stubborn. It's not too late to go back to the university,' Tuấn said.

Bình stared at the road. Tuấn hadn't commented, but they had driven well past their destination, Springvale. In fact, if he kept going, they would reach the university. But he used to take the train there. Students like him didn't have cars. When he started working at Cô Năm's grocery shop this summer, Uncle Ba lent him some money to put a deposit on a car. The shop was close to home, but the car was useful when Cô Năm wanted him to go to other grocery stores at seven in the evening to pick up the cartons of green soya milk and fermented pork patty that were cheaper because they were about to expire. Piece of shit though it was, the Commodore was the most expensive thing Bình owned and it cemented his withdrawal from university.

'Why aren't *you* in school, then?'

Tuấn snorted.

'You know why, man. I can't do that stuff. School. Even before seventy-five, I was already running tables at Năm Vương. But you were gonna be a teacher.'

Bình hated it when his friends referred so casually to

Vietnam before the war ended, before the Fall of Saigon, as if that event were just another mark on the timeline.

'Well, like you, then,' he said. 'I got sick of it. I mean it! They all think they're better than us. I don't need that shit. Look, I've got a steady job working with our people. I'll save a little bit, trade in this shitty car. I can play pool, drink with you and the boys, do whatever I want.'

Bình had never told Tuấn about the broken chair. He had been struggling at university for three months. The classwork wasn't the problem. It was hard, but he was getting on top of it. No matter what he did, however, he couldn't get rid of his Vietnamese accent. Students talked to him only when they had to, loudly and slowly. Mortified, he would watch their thin lips stretch grotesquely as they dragged out each word, their eyes widening, questioning: 'Do. You. Understand?' One day he spat into one of those faces. Tony Chillinski's. Tony swung an arm to push Bình back. Not expecting the strength of the meaty palms, Bình staggered, then lunged forward to drive his elbow into the big man's stomach.

The counsellor was even worse. His obvious pity enraged Bình, who smashed a chair in the counselling office against the desk.

'It's different,' Tuấn said. 'I mean, I *couldn't* be in school, I don't have the brains. You could do it, but what the fuck are you doing instead? Stacking shelves with freeze-dried noodles and greasing off every white man who walks past the shop.'

'Fuck you. So what if I could? I don't *want* to. I don't like it. You know what I get stacking shelves? Freedom. Nobody looks down on me there, I'm nobody's fool.'

In his peripheral vision, Bình saw Tuấn pick up the copy of *To Kill a Mockingbird* off the seat. Disgusted, he met Tuấn's gaze, lunged sideways and, in a split second, snatched the book and threw it out the window. He saw the pages in his mind's eye, already loosened by the spine he had broken four years ago, tearing apart and littering the freeway with Scout's overalls and Boo's metaphors.

They didn't speak again for another long stretch of road. On top of his self-loathing, Bình now felt ashamed that Tuấn had to suffer his company. He eyed the petrol gauge, calculating the hours he'd need to put in at the store to pay for this reckless drive. He wanted to explain. He had been trying to explain ever since they left Bidong, hadn't he?

'Even back in the refugee camp, they didn't treat us like this,' Bình said haltingly. He felt like crying. 'Because they didn't expect us to be like them. They only expected us to be us. But here. At a university where white people go to learn how to fucking be older white people, I...'

He slammed his palm on the dashboard again.

'I used to go running every morning around the camp. In the stinking hot, bare feet, empty stomach. Fuck knows, no one could afford runners. I thought I should keep fit, you know? Because I wanted to be going somewhere to make myself better.'

His knuckles strained against the steering wheel. He imagined his bone ripping through his skin.

'Let's go,' Tuấn said.

'What?'

'Let's go running. Take the next exit and we can head back into town, to the Alexandra Gardens. There's this great running track that goes for miles and miles around the park.'

'No way. That's so fucking white,' Bình said, recalling the paths filled with women in bright sports bras and yoga pants, old men with hairy chests and sagging bellies, businessmen in silky sports clothes, carrying designer water bottles.

'Nobody owns running, man. It's just running.'

'Doesn't feel right.'

'No, fuck you.' Tuấn was smiling. 'What could be more right than two guys going running because they feel like it?'

More to please Tuấn than anything, Bình drove to the Alexandra Gardens and parked next to the running track. Their old T-shirts and daggy fleece trousers were for work or home, but it seemed the wrong time to talk about clothes. Nervous, they didn't say much as they got out of the car and started jogging. They didn't know anyone who ran around the gardens in Melbourne. Bình was right: only white people did it.

But no one looked at them twice and Bình started to enjoy the sensations of his body finding a running rhythm. It had been a long time since he had done any exercise; his lungs felt constricted and his calves stiff. He turned to look at his friend before they both picked up the pace.

The gardens were well maintained and the sandy paths easy to run on. Moving through the cool shadows of evening felt like a long sigh of relief.

They didn't continue for long; both men were unused to exercise. After half an hour, they were back in the car, panting. Bình fished out two cans of Coke from the back seat. He pulled the tab on his can and it clicked and hissed just like in the ads.

'Shit, that's warm,' Tuấn said, taking a sip. 'Remember when these things were so precious?'

'Chị Hai used to hide Coke cans in the shelf behind the family altar,' Bình said, picturing their old apartment in Sài Gòn, so small it didn't have many secret places.

'That sounds just like your sister,' said Tuấn, chuckling.

'Three or four cans, hot as this,' continued Bình, 'sitting behind the statues and incense for months at a time. We shared a can sometimes, when our parents were out. Chị Hai liked to drink one before going on a date. I used to tell her: you should make your boyfriends buy you real Cokes, cold and fresh at the shop.'

Bình smiled, remembering Chị Hai's haughty response: 'Please. My boys can't afford one can between them, the fucking druggos.' She said it just to amuse him. Back then, she was dating a teacher who doted on her and brought fruit for the family whenever he visited.

'And the peanut butter! Remember?' Tuấn exclaimed.

Relaxed now, Bình nodded enthusiastically.

'Nothing like American peanut butter!' Tuấn said. 'One of my buddies was selling stuff from the American soldier packs for a while. Stolen? Left behind? I don't know. Wow, all of it was so good. Peanut butter and spam. You ever tried spam before seventy-five?'

'Yeah.'

'So good, huh? I reckon nothing ever tasted so good to me as American peanut butter and spam. Definitely not the peanut butter here. Why can't the Australians get it right? Tastes like fucking plastic here. Spam's still the same, though. Good as ever.'

'You love spam way too much.'

'Nothing wrong with a can of spam, man.'

'It's gonna give you a heart attack someday.'

'Nah, come on. Look at me,' Tuấn flipped up his shirt and smacked his stomach. 'Nothing sticks.'

Tuấn lived alone. If Bình was there for dinner, he served fried spam on rice, along with a cucumber, a red chilli from the neighbour's bush and a Carlton Draught.

'Hey, man, what are we gonna do for dinner? It's so late,' Tuấn said. Instantly, Bình felt the banality of their daily lives return: eat quickly, sleep, wake up early to get to work.

'I've got food at home,' Bình said as he turned on the ignition.

The sight of the freeway made Bình anxious again. The white dashes on the road emerged, then flew out of sight, leaping into the dark blue sky. Bình wondered if he would ever get used to this much space, speed, and all those neat white lines. It was the antithesis of his memory of Vietnam, the unlined roads, the intersections crowded with riders tottering on motorbikes that could only inch forward in the tangle of traffic, their helmets and facemasks dotted with tacky, colourful patterns.

Bình curled his fingers around the steering wheel to brace

himself. He felt childish. The satisfaction he'd got from the run was already leaving him, and the spectre of loneliness loomed again.

'Hey,' he said to Tuấn.

'Yeah?'

Bình tapped his fingers on the wheel, not sure what to say.

'We should get some new music,' he muttered.

'Yeah. What do you want?'

'Is the new *Paris by Night* out?' Bình asked.

'Oh yeah, the tenth anniversary show. I reckon Bắc Ánh should have a copy by the weekend,' said Tuấn.

They got most of their videos from Bắc Ánh, who ran a pirated tapes business out of his house.

'Hey.'

'What?'

'Want to come to dinner at Chị Hai's this Sunday?'

'Of course, you know I love her cooking.'

'It's my mother's death anniversary.'

'I wouldn't miss it, man.'

It was eleven by the time they got back to Bình's place in Springvale, a portable room in his aunt and uncle's backyard. He had a small fridge and a microwave, but no stove. Bình found a box of Chị Hai's *thịt kho*, braised pork and boiled eggs in sauce, and some old rice, and heated it up in the microwave. They ate on the patio furniture in the backyard, speaking softly so as not to wake Bình's Aunt Ba and Uncle Ba. After Tuấn had left to walk home, only a few streets away, Bình stayed sitting in the backyard. Over the fence he heard a neighbour's screen door squeak open, steps into the backyard, the thump of the plastic bin swinging open, *whump*, as the garbage bag went in, faint chatter inside the house.

He was much more nervous about Sunday's dinner than Tuấn knew. Chị Hai hadn't seen or spoken to him since their fight about him leaving university, although she still sent him food through Uncle Ba. He had known she wouldn't take the news well and had been too afraid to tell her himself. When she heard it from Uncle Ba, she drove over, after picking up her daughter, Yến, from school. Yến was made to sit in the house while Chị Hai talked to Bình in the backyard. She burst into tears, called him disobedient, selfish, an embarrassment to the family. She yelled at him as if he were a child, even though she was only four years older.

'You never think of anybody but yourself. Don't you understand that we have to work twice as hard, grit our teeth twice as much? You have brains but you're dumb, Bình.'

Her voice cracked and then she hissed:

'Sometimes I feel like you don't understand how much I love you. You think I like working two restaurant jobs? You think it's nice for me? You think everybody is kind to me there? No, I do it so that you can study and make something of yourself. It breaks my heart to love you this way, Bình. It breaks my heart, and my arms, and my back.'

'*Thôi đi*,' he shouted: *Enough*. 'If you don't like it, then stop. Nobody's asking you to break your back.'

She stormed into the house.

They had the same temper. Standing on the other side of

the slammed door, he had glared down at his pale, clenched fists.

They had lived together when they came to Australia five years ago. Sometimes they sat all night on the carpet with a pot of food between them (always an onion omelette if it was his turn to cook), watching Australian TV, making fun of the words and imitating the stiff, bragging style of game-show hosts. Some nights she brought back egg tarts from the Chinese restaurant where she worked. When he had a test coming up, she bought a glass of three-bean drink, his favou-rite, with a little bag of shaved iced, and another bag of thick coconut milk to pour over the beans. Even at the beginning of her courtship with Long, she was still lighthearted. She made horrified faces at Bình's impressions of Long, like the way he began a sentence loudly and angrily, and confused himself halfway through. She swatted Bình on the head, and they fought and laughed the way they always had as children. Now her face went dark whenever Bình said the slightest thing to mock Long.

Bình's mind filled with images of carefree young Chị Hai and disapproving older Chị Hai. He blinked and looked around. The neighbours were quiet now. Tuấn's company had kept his loneliness at bay, but he knew it was returning. He had to get inside, away from the still grass lawn, the old hose and the view of fences and roofs. The quietness was terrifying: it haunted him with the fear that he lived in an unoccupied world.

Cô Năm picked a fight on Friday. Bình had spent the morning unpacking a new shipment and stacking the freezer. He was sitting outside on a green crate, having a cigarette break, when he heard her screeching.

'*Bình! Where is he? Bình, Bình, Bình, Bình, Bình, Bình, Bình!*' she screamed, until she found him. She grabbed his forearm, her long manicured nails digging into his flesh, and dragged him up.

'What?' he shook his arm out of her grip.

'You underdeveloped motherfucker,' Cô Năm snarled. 'Do you enjoy stealing from me? Are you here to steal from me, boy?'

He bristled, trying not to respond, trying to think of her as pathetic rather than evil. He knew he must not lash out as he had in his first week there, when both his aunt and uncle had to plead with Cô Năm to let him keep his job. He looked down at her, a squat woman in her forties, with rings of fat on her stubby arms like a baby's. Last month, she came back from Vietnam with freshly tattooed eyebrows, eyeliner and lipliner. Bình wondered why so many Vietnamese immigrant women did it. He found Cô Năm's lipliner horrifying: it hadn't fully healed by the time she came back and her whole mouth was swollen, the bottom lip thick and protruding. Now she had on dark-red tattoo lipliner without lipstick, and the outlines did not match the lines of her mouth.

'What are you looking at me like that for, you insolent boy? This boy has problems. I swear this boy will kill me in 'my sleep!' she declared, glancing back at her husband, Chú Phụng, who was skulking inside between the aisles.

'I'm sorry, what's wrong?' Bình kept his tone measured.

'*I'm sorry, what's wrong,*' she pronounced in a mock-sophisticated Hà Nội accent, even though Bình had a Sài Gòn accent. 'What's *wrong* is that you took in ten boxes of king prawns when the order was for fifteen. You think you can steal from me, but you're not as *smart* as you think you are.'

'I checked the order. It was right.'

'Do I look scared to you? You think because you went to university that I will be scared of you?'

'No, that's not what I think. I checked all the orders,' Bình said.

'What's this about?' Chú Phụng emerged from the shop, looking exhausted as usual.

'This boy...' Cô Năm began.

'Let's just check the orders, shall we?' Chú Phụng said. 'Come inside. Come on. Here. King prawns. Fifteen.'

'*It is always fifteen,*' Cô Năm said shrilly.

'All right. And now we check with the supplier,' said Chú Phụng, closing the notebook and reaching for his address book. Bình could not remember a time in his life when he had been so bored, or done any job so poorly. He didn't care about the work. It was meaningless and Cô Năm hated him.

'This is Phụng at Phat Tai groceries in Springvale,' Chú Phụng said into the phone. 'Yes, yes. I'm good, thanks, I hope your family is well. Good, good.'

Bình idly ran his hand against the boxes of Pocky behind

him. He wasn't the best worker, it was true, and often snacked on the produce when Cô Năm was out, but he was just like most of the young workers at these Viet/Chinese groceries: bored, lazy and sullen. Self-important managers like Cô Năm ran the shops, getting rich, or at least richer than the other Vietnamese, who waited tables or worked in factories.

'King prawns—yes, king prawns,' said Chú Phụng. 'I see. That's fine. No, just the refund. Thank you. Good.'

'Well?' Cô Năm demanded.

'They delivered ten instead of fifteen.'

'They're always trying to cheat us!' Cô Năm shouted. 'Those dirty motherfuckers.'

She rounded on Bình, pinching his upper arm.

'And you, *idiot* boy, you want to lose all my money? No wonder the university kicked you out. What good are you if you can't even count?'

Bình wrenched his arm away. Her eyes grew wide.

'*What*? Are you *mad*? Are you going to *hit me?*' she goaded.

'All right,' Chú Phụng said dryly. 'You are giving me a headache. Everything's figured out. Bình, check carefully next time, okay?'

'Okay.'

Bing was increasingly frightened that his boredom with the job was corroding his mind. When he checked the shipping documents, he took nothing in; he could no longer figure out the smallest details. Even at home, when he looked at newspapers, he felt exhausted by the words.

He began stacking the sweet drinks in rows along the

freezer. He peeked through the cans and saw Cô Năm behind the counter. She had settled onto her stool and was holding the phone to her ear. Every day she spoke for hours on the phone with her relatives in Vietnam. The shop never had much business until three in the afternoon, when people came home from work. There was no trace on Cô Năm's face now of the drama that had just transpired.

Bình's hands were going numb from the frost on the cans. He stared at the pale, disembodied fingers. He kept stacking.

He met Tuấn at Café Saigon after work. Tuấn finished the lunch shift at three and had a dinner shift starting at six on Fridays, so he stayed at the café. He was watching a soccer game with two of their friends, Quân and Trịnh. Their glasses of black iced coffee had turned watery.

'Hey, look at these guys. Soccer, now that's one of the games where us Asians can actually compete with white guys,' said Tuấn.

'That South Korean team is awful,' said Bình.

'Yeah, but at least they get to play.'

'No Vietnamese up there, that's for sure,' said Quân.

'South Koreans got it figured out way better than us. We should've split the country when we could've,' said Trịnh.

'Who could've, huh? Your skinny ass?' said Tuấn.

'But seriously. We almost had a Korean deal going on,' Trịnh persisted. 'Bình, you're the scholar. What went wrong?'

'What do you think the rest of us are, apes?' said Quân.

'Everyone knows Vietnam was partitioned into North and South.'

'Yeah, but I mean it even happened the same year as Korea split. Paris conference in fifty-four,' said Trịnh.

'Geneva,' Bình corrected him. His ice coffee had finished filtering, and he was mixing in the condensed milk. He didn't like drinking it black like the other guys did. He had a sweet tooth. 'They talked about Vietnam in Geneva, but they only split up Korea. They couldn't decide on Vietnam.'

'You dumb-ass,' Quân said to Trịnh.

'Right, right,' Trịnh snapped. 'Paris was where the Americans started backing out.'

'Yeah…' muttered Bình.

'Yeah, well. I bet a South Vietnam soccer team would have a better chance than the Vietnam team,' said Trịnh.

'Come on. The Vietnam team is basically the North Vietnam team,' said Quân.

'Whatever,' said Tuấn. 'No Asian team can go up against the white guys. Look, look how big that one is.' He lunged at the screen.

'Size doesn't matter in soccer.'

'You need power behind the kick, though. And when they pile on top of each other. You think a little Asian man is going to come out alive?'

'I reckon I'd like to be South Korean. You know all the women in Vietnam want to marry a Korean now?' said Trịnh. 'One of my sister's friends just ran off on her fiancé for a South Korean guy she hadn't even met before.'

'It's because they're all watching South Korean shows now,' said Quân.

Bình looked at the TV without focusing. He liked the guys, but he wasn't in the mood for their inane talk. Tuấn was his only real friend.

'Bình, Bình,' Tuấn said after a while. 'Are you pissed off about something?'

Bình looked around self-consciously.

'Ah, nothing. Trouble at work again. My manager, you know.'

'Tell me about it,' said Quân. 'My manager is so fucking racist. He makes all the Viet guys do the loading, and all the Chinese guys just fiddle with these machines at the belt.'

Bình was instantly annoyed that Quân had made the conversation about him.

'He says Viet guys are stronger.' Trịnh chuckled.

Trịnh and Quân were both stocky men and avid eaters. They had come to the café straight from the factory floor, wearing dusty navy coveralls, the sleeves rolled up. Their forearms popped with thick veins. Tuấn and Bình, on the other hand, were regarded as too skinny and too feminine respectively, although the guys had long stopped making fun of Bình, after his angry outbursts.

'I think he means dumber,' said Quân. 'But seriously, it's because they won't fucking work otherwise. The Chinese are cheats. They cheat when a manager's not looking, so they've got to be inside, under the manager's nose. Only we can do the loading.'

'You think that's bad,' Tuấn joined in. 'I'm paid less than the Chinese guys at the restaurant. I get seven bucks an hour, they get ten.'

'Tuấn, that's because the Chinese guys at your restaurant are the manager's family,' said Quân.

'But fuck that, there's a fifteen-year-old Chinese kid getting paid more than me.'

'You should've been Chinese, huh,' said Quân.

'I'd take Korean over Chinese any day.'

'Stop shitting on Viet guys. We don't get it so bad,' said Tuấn.

'What do we get?'

'We have beautiful women,' Tuấn offered.

'Okay, where are they? Where's your beautiful woman?' Quân challenged.

The men were all single and worried about not finding a wife. They joked about being alone so Bình assumed they did not feel the same kind of haunted loneliness that he did. But he was convinced that no one could enjoy living alone in these suburbs, with the crippling quiet and the parched lawns.

'Quỳnh!' Tuấn said to the woman wiping the table across from them. 'Look, here she is. Here's my most beautiful woman.'

Quỳnh, a thirty-something woman with pretty eyes, a fringe and ponytail, and wearing rubber flip-flops, sauntered over and flung a tea towel onto their table.

'Fuck your mother, Tuấn. Are you guys going to order something or just keep stinking up my shop?'

'What's the matter, Quỳnh? Don't you see I just want to spend time with you?' said Tuấn.

'Hey, Quỳnh,' said Trịnh. 'Are you into Korean guys?'

'There are no Koreans in Australia.'

'I mean on the screen. You watch the Korean shows?'

'I'm a TVB girl, the Hong Kong actors are much more handsome,' she said. She shifted onto one hip. There were no other customers in the shop. If they talked to her long enough, she would probably bring out a dish of something that was getting cold.

'Talk about Hong Kong!' Trịnh exclaimed. '*That's* the best. Really modern, independent, rich.'

'We shoulda made a Hong Kong kind of deal with China,' said Quân.

'You mean with North Vietnam,' said Trịnh.

Quân laughed dryly. 'The North Vietnam team basically *is* the Chinese team.'

Bình scraped his chair back on the concrete. Everyone stopped talking and looked at him.

'I gotta go, got to pick up some things … for Sunday,' Bình muttered.

No one said anything. Bình wondered angrily if Tuấn had discussed Bình's problems with them.

'Bình! Drinks at mine tonight, you coming?' Quân called out to him as he was leaving.

'Ah, maybe, yeah, I'll see,' Bình said, though he had no intention of turning up.

'Where's my invite?' he heard Quỳnh saying as he walked

off. It was a joke. Quỳnh wouldn't go and they wouldn't want her to. Quân and Trịnh lived in a share house with four other single Vietnamese men. The drinking nights were sloppy affairs, from which the married men came home to angry wives, skipped the next drinking night, then came to the one after, desperate to maintain a veneer of independence.

Bình went home and spent the rest of the night watching TV. At one point, he picked up a second-hand copy of *Black Beauty*. He knew it would take him a long time to sleep. The days never seemed to end anymore. He felt as if there was something important to do, but there never was.

On Sunday morning, he drove Aunt Ba to buy flowers for Chị Hai. Uncle Ba slept in on Sundays. They were a quiet couple, and timid with Bình since they had witnessed his temper. When he first moved in with them, after Chị Hai got married, he spent most of his time watching TV in the living room. Aunt Ba had been unable to find work in Australia, and seemed to be compensating with unnecessary vigour in her housework. Every morning at six, she started scrubbing and then sweeping the tiled floors, before vacuuming the carpet in the living room. After a breakfast break—instant coffee and some sort of sweet bun—she began the daily chore of washing and drying the sheets. Then she wiped the bathroom and kitchen until they were spotless. Once the cleaning was finished, she began the cooking.

One day, soon after he'd arrived, Aunt Ba asked him to move off the couch.

'Can't you do the couch later?' He was watching a *Paris by Night* comedy sketch.

'It won't take long.'

'Just vacuum something else first and do the couch later.'

She looked at him, shocked. 'No,' she said, confused. She patted the couch twice.

'Stop pestering me. Just rest until the show is over! What?' Now she looked frightened.

'Relax! What's wrong?' he shouted at her. 'People are going to think you've gone crazy.'

She left and shut herself in her bedroom. That evening, Uncle Ba came to talk to him—as the brother of Bình's mother, he was the blood relative. He was a short, quiet man, afraid of conflict. The couple was not close to anyone, but they were careful about fulfilling their spiritual and familial duties: they sent monthly remittances to family members, went to temple once a week and made donations there.

'We welcomed you to our house because you are family.' Uncle Ba pushed his glasses nervously up his nose. 'But you have not been kind to us. You upset your aunt very much. The way you spoke to her was disrespectful. You should have been helping her with the housework rather than yelling at her.'

'It was a mistake. I promise it won't happen again.'

Uncle Ba shook his head. 'We know you have problems, Bình. Your aunt is a very gentle woman, she cannot stand violence. You have to change your ways.'

Bình retreated to his room more and more. Eventually Aunt Ba and Uncle Ba stopped asking him to come in for dinner. Chị Hai sent him food so he knew she must have had a conversation with them about his behaviour—that irritated him too.

Aunt Ba and Uncle Ba were not close to Chị Hai either, but it was their familial duty to come to the Sunday lunch.

'Do you know what flowers your sister likes?' Aunt Ba asked as they entered the florist.

'Sunflowers are her favourite.'

'Sunflowers would be inappropriate,' Aunt Ba muttered.

'She also likes birds of paradise.'

Bình remembered Chị Hai discovering the strange, elegant flower one day in a real-estate office: a single flower in a skinny white vase, surrounded by thick green leaves. Chị Hai had laughed and ruffled the orange-and-purple crown of the flower. 'Somebody tried to make the world very perfect,' she said.

'That's too expensive,' said Aunt Ba, as she picked out a bunch of white lilies.

Back home, she continued making *nem*, pork skewers, to bring to Chị Hai's. Uncle Ba was working in the garden, having refused Bình's help. They were going to drive over to Chị Hai's at three o'clock. Feeling agitated from the interactions with his aunt and uncle, Bình waited in his room, a Jackie Chan movie on in the background.

He had to wait until ten to three before picking up Tuấn. He didn't want to arrive before his aunt and uncle. Tuấn was waiting outside his place, standing at the kerb, holding a bag of mangoes for Chị Hai. They had a cigarette before they drove off.

'Are you still sad?' Tuấn asked.

Bình started. 'What?'

'About your mother's death.'

'Oh. No, it's been a long time.'

'You're lucky, though,' said Tuấn. 'You have family with you here.'

Bình winced. His stomach churned all the way to Chị Hai's place, a twenty-minute drive to Glen Waverly. It was more of a Chinese neighbourhood, but Chị Hai wanted to be in the Glen Waverly High School catchment zone for Yến. Their new house was smaller, another reason Bình had to move out. The other reason was Long.

Chị Hai opened the door, her right hand in a pink rubber glove covered in chicken guts. She wore a bright orange shirt and slacks. Her hair was tied in a bun and there was blush on her cheeks. She greeted Aunt Ba and Uncle Ba cheerfully and hugged Tuấn. Tuấn had always admired Chị Hai, and often joked with her about how much he wanted her to marry him instead of Long.

'Any excuse to see you. You look beautiful,' said Tuấn.

People usually gravitated toward Chị Hai because she was cheerful, talkative and kind. But today Chị Hai looked as if she was on the verge of tears. Feeling hopeless, Bình just nodded at her and followed the others into the kitchen.

Yến ran to greet him and he gave her a hug before slinging her over his shoulder. Everyone helped with the anniversary preparations. Aunt Ba went straight to her task, peeling and chopping vegetables at the kitchen bench. Tuấn and Bình ferried food and utensils from the kitchen to the altar table, which had to be set up as though three people were about to eat at it—mother, grandfather and grandmother, whose portraits were on Chi's altar. The best food went to the altar: the neatest spring rolls, grilled *nem* decorated with chili, rice noodle strips laid out in a grid pattern and covered with a spoonful of scallion oil, and the best mangoes. Long went to set up the folding table and chairs in the backyard. Yến sat at the kitchen bench wrapping wontons as carefully as she could.

'I'd really like a family,' said Tuấn, not for the first time. 'I'd throw great Sunday dinners. I'd cook with my wife. You know, I'm actually very good at cooking, I just never get the chance to.'

'I'll believe it when I see it,' said Bình.

'You could come. Bring your wife, when you find one. We could have more kids running around. Yến must get lonely,' said Tuấn, looking over at the little girl.

Suddenly they heard a commotion in the backyard, and the sound of clattering metal. Tuấn and Bình went to look through the glass sliding door. Long had kicked over a chair. Chị Hai stood before him. A plate of rice noodles had fallen onto the concrete, the china in shards among the noodles.

'Please behave, Long,' Chị Hai begged in a small voice.

Bình went to the kitchen bench to stand with Yến, who was listening intently.

'What is it with you? I don't see you working this hard for

237

my family's events,' shouted Long. 'And take that stuff off your face. You look like a fool.'

Chị Hai's voice was too low for Bình to hear.

'Enough!' Long threw another chair out of his way. More clattering. 'I'm going for a smoke.'

No one moved until they heard Long's engine ignite and the car drive away.

Then Chị Hai laughed nervously.

'He just needs a break,' she said to Uncle Ba. She scooped up the noodles with her hands and rushed into the house to the rubbish bin. 'He gets stressed with these events.'

Yến went over and tugged on her arm.

'Come on, we have work to do. Look, there's so much wonton filling left,' said Chị Hai with forced enthusiasm.

They continued the preparations in silence. Once the altar dishes were ready and a large watermelon was set up in pride of place, flanked by mangoes, everybody took turns to light incense and pray. Bình gazed at the portrait of his mother, tracing Chị's features in hers. He wanted to reminisce with Chị Hai, but they hadn't reconciled.

Chị Hai had made another dish for eating, not as an offering—egg noodles with chicken. Yến's favourite. They ate quickly, thankful for the distraction of food. Bình wondered when Long would come back. At the end of the meal, their Aunt Ba and Uncle Ba announced that they were leaving.

'We get tired now, getting old, you know.' Uncle Ba chuckled half-heartedly. 'And work tomorrow... It was a really wonderful dinner, dear.'

Chị Hai pressed some noodles and *nem* onto them before they left. She told Tuấn to put on the new *Paris by Night* tape he had brought, and left him and Yến in the living room, while Bình did the dishes.

Bình was uncomfortable seeing his confident sister falter. It wasn't the first time he had witnessed fighting between her and Long. He felt paralysed. Chị Hai was always wise, did everything well, pleased everybody. Bình needed to believe that her life was good, that she was happy—even when she was yelling at him. She had always been in control, and he'd always been able to talk to her. Until now. He knew he couldn't bring up Long; they had already had so many fights about him. Bình dropped the dishes back into the sink and went to find her.

She was in the bathroom, the door open, wiping the make-up off her face.

'Bình,' she said gently. She splashed water on her face and dried her hands, then laughed.

'Don't be worried about me,' she said. 'I wanted to talk to you about something.'

He was relieved. Her vulnerability had scared him. He followed her into the bedroom, where she knelt in front of the drawers by her bed and took out an envelope. She sat down and patted the carpet in front of her. Bình sat down.

'I'm not going to push you into anything anymore. I just want to say that you still have the option of going back to the university. I collected *hụi* last week—I'd been planning it for months—so there's money if you want to go back,' she said.

Chị Hai was a dedicated player of *hụi*, a rotating credit association with an annual cashout for each contributor.

'You're not angry at me anymore?'

'Of course I'm angry. Of course I am,' she said disdainfully. 'But I realise there's nothing I can do about it.'

She brought her hand to her face, as if she was going to wipe away tears, but instead she massaged her right cheek. She had changed out of her good clothes into the cheap cotton pyjamas she wore at home. Bình wasn't sure what to say.

'No, I haven't changed my mind,' she continued. 'My work is hard, Bình. It doesn't lead anywhere, it just gets me through day by day, and that's a hard way to live. You haven't worked long enough to dread this kind of work.' She sucked her breath in shallowly. 'I need something to look forward to, or I don't know if I can keep doing this. University, and a better job, was never going to happen for me, but you could really study, I know you could. But now I'm scolding you again. Maybe I'm forcing you, just for my own sake, just for something for me to hope for. That's not fair on you.'

The talk of dread scared him. It hadn't been easy for him to leave the university. There was certainly a lot to dread there too. He had imagined that he would be more at peace if he did something safe, contained and free of ambition, like the grocery job. But he had come to fear it in a different way.

'I don't think I've been happy anywhere here. I haven't been happy since we left home,' he admitted. 'Since we left Sài Gòn.'

Finally he told her everything as best he could. He wanted her to know the feeling of looking out at the lawns and fences and roofs, how he panicked sometimes with the conviction that there was no one else in the world. How sometimes he wanted to wake his aunt or uncle, even though he knew they didn't care, just to hear a human voice. At night he dreaded the coming of the next day, dreaded waking up in the morning. And Australia in winter was so cold, especially in the mornings, when he was overcome by the realisation that there was nothing he wanted here, nothing at all. Perhaps they should never have left Vietnam. It was a strange migration that he still hadn't figured out. He seemed to have left the destiny prepared for him, slipped out of it, and now there was nothing waiting for him at all.

More than ten years ago, when he had tested into Tiểu Văn Bình, the selective politics school in Sài Gòn, Chị Hai saved money from selling pressed coconut pancakes and took him to eat *phở* to celebrate. When he then failed the health test because he was five kilos underweight and couldn't enrol, she wept so inconsolably that he kicked the tower of cosmetics she had arranged in a corner to sell out of the apartment.

He looked at her now and thought that if he didn't love her, there would be so little to care for in his life. He knew it would be dumb and childish, but he desperately needed an answer.

'Chị Hai, do you think something good is going to happen?'

She reached out for Bình's hand and held it between her own two hands. Her grip wasn't as firm as it used to be. Her eyes were shining, her lips twisted in anguish, and Bình felt a rush of love for his sister, who understood how scared and sad he was, and who would carry all of it with her.

Acknowledgments

To the Literature Department at New York University Abu Dhabi, especially my mentor Deborah Williams, who asked me the important questions; John Coughlin, who always inexplicably believed in me; Bryan Waterman, for making lit cool from day one; Werner Sollors, for making me feel heard; and Jim Savio, who wouldn't let me give up.

To my family for telling me stories. For the hardships they went through so that I could be here and know this language and create this book. Especially Mum, for answering emergency phone calls about what materials were used to make buckets for carrying water from wells in 1960s rural Vietnam, and for everything.

Cho gia đình thân yêu của Duyên. Vì những khổ cực mà gia đình phải vượt qua để Duyên có ngày hôm nay, để Duyên biết Tiếng Anh, và để Duyên hoàn thành cuốn sách này. Hơn ai hết, Duyên biết ơn mẹ, vì mẹ đã trả lời bao cuộc gọi khẩn của Duyên về vật liệu làm thùng xách nước giếng ở miền quê Việt Nam hồi những năm 60, và vì tất cả.

To my friends, my inner circle, who read this book in its earliest form as copies that were sewn together by hand.

To the Text Publishing team for making my dream come

true. To my editor Penny Hueston for her wisdom and patience in improving my writing. To Jamila, Kate, Shalini, and Jess for their wonderful work.

To Bram Presser, for giving me a lucky ticket to this book.